With special thanks to David Grant

Also in the

series:

Canyon Chaos

Rainforest Rampage

Arctic Adventure

AXEL LEWIS
ROBOT RACES
DESERT DISASTER

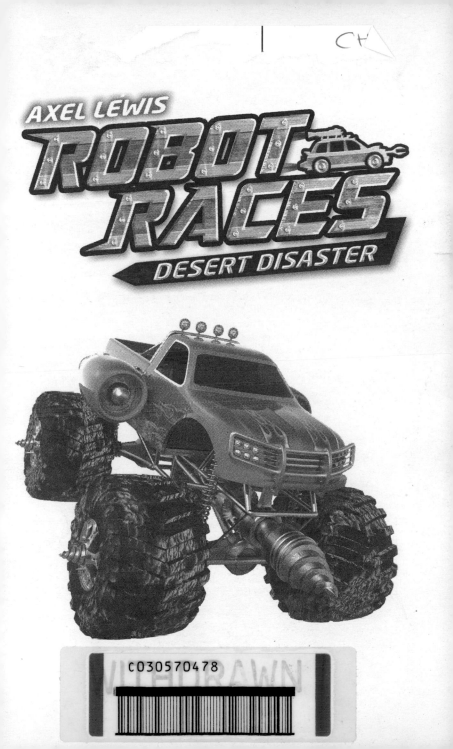

First published in 2013 by Curious Fox,
an imprint of Capstone Global Library Limited,
7 Pilgrim Street, London, EC4V 6LB
Registered company number: 6695582

www.curious-fox.com

Text © Hothouse Fiction Ltd 2013

Series created by Hothouse Fiction
www.hothousefiction.com

The author's moral rights are hereby asserted.

Cover illustration by Spooky Pooka
Cover design by Mandy Norman

ISBN 978 1 78202 051 6

1 3 5 7 9 10 8 6 4 2

A CIP catalogue for this book is available from the British Library.

Typeset in Avenir by Hothouse Fiction Ltd

Printed and bound by CPI Group (UK) Ltd, Croydon, CR0 4YY

MIX
Paper from
responsible sources
FSC® C020471
FSC
www.fsc.org

CHAPTER ONE
Up in the Air

"On your marks ... get set ... *go!*" shouted Princess Kako.

Jimmy Roberts reached for a packet of crisps from the table and popped it open with one hand. Beside him, Chip Travers did the same.

Opposite them sat Missy McGovern and Sammy Bahur, each with their hands clasped behind their backs and their mouths open wide like two seals at feeding time.

"Incoming!" Jimmy shouted to Missy as he started throwing salty crisps at her mouth as quickly as he could, while Chip did the same to Sammy. The crisps were bouncing off noses, ears and cheeks as Missy and Sammy weaved to and fro, fighting to catch as many in their mouths as they could.

"Come on, Sammy," yelled Chip. "We can't afford to lose this game."

"Iiimm-ooeein-mmiii-eeeessss!" the Egyptian boy replied, which Jimmy decided must translate into, *"I'm doing my best!"*

"Time's up," said Kako suddenly. "Everybody stop what you are doing. Close your mouths and put down the snacks!"

The room fell silent apart from the dull noise of food being chewed.

"I think we won that one, don't you, Jimmy?" said Missy, shaking crumbs from her hair.

"Are you kidding me?" said Chip. "We caught more chips than you! Kako, who won?"

"I was too busy laughing!" the Japanese princess replied.

Jimmy smiled and shook his head as the jokey squabble carried on. Missy had come up with the game and it had had the entire group laughing the whole way through their lunch hour.

Jimmy plucked a sandwich from the table and popped it into his mouth. He was reaching for his drink when he noticed that the liquid in the glass was tilting at a funny angle. It was the only sign that he was actually suspended thousands of metres in the air on an enormous airship owned by none other than the famous billionaire Lord Ludwick Leadpipe. The water rolled up the right side of his drinking glass ever so slightly as the giant craft moved through the air.

Jimmy loved being part of the first-ever Robot Races for kids. He loved the danger, the excitement and visiting new places. But the competition had become so popular that all the racers had turned into celebrities overnight. All of a sudden, newspaper reporters wanted to know everything about them, and had started standing on their doorsteps with camera crews day and night to catch a glimpse here and a quick word there. Grandpa had got so fed up with them turning up at his door that he'd rigged the doorbell to squirt water at whoever rang it!

Soon Lord Leadpipe had decided to take action. He converted part of his giant airship into a school, and gathered everyone on board to live there for the duration of the Races.

The luxury airliner had everything – luxury en-suite cabins, a fancy restaurant, cinema, a bowling alley, classrooms, science labs, and a canteen that was bigger than the one at Jimmy's school. Leadpipe had hired a tutor to teach them all the usual subjects like maths and science, but he'd also arranged for them to be taught a few *special* lessons. They were being taught basic mechanics, advanced driving skills and interview techniques – all things they'd need to be top robot racers.

Looking around the table at the other competitors, Jimmy still couldn't believe he was now living aboard a giant airship. It was completely different from the run-down house in Smedingham where he had been brought up by his grandpa. The same grandpa who had also turned out to be a genius robot inventor and engineer – when he wasn't busy being a taxi driver.

Around Jimmy were the other robot racers. They were all kids like him, taking part in the biggest, most exciting tournament the world had ever seen – each with their own robot equipped with the finest gadgets and technology. They were friends now, but on the track they'd be fighting each other for first place.

First there was Princess Kako from Japan. She and her robobike, Lightning, were serious contenders in the Robot Races championship, having already won one stage of the competition. Lightning was light and fast, usually shaped like a motorbike – although he could transform into lots of other vehicles when needed – and was propelled by two turbo jets.

Next came Chip Travers. Chip's racer was called Dug, and he was a giant diggerbot with a large hydraulic arm that had come in handy a few times in the tournament. They'd been friends since Jimmy had rescued Chip from the Grand Canyon in their first race together.

Opposite Chip sat Samir – or Sammy, as he liked to be called – a skinny boy from Egypt who came from a long line of successful racing drivers. His father, Omar Bahur, had been a champion robot racer in his day, leaving Sammy a lot to live up to. His robot was called Maximus, and was a huge hovercraft able to glide at top speed on a cushion of air.

"I have never seen such arguments over a snack before," whispered Sammy to Jimmy as Missy and

Chip continued their debate. "It is almost as if this game is as important as the Robot Races, no?"

Jimmy laughed. "I think we're all a bit *competitive*, Sammy."

Missy turned to the two of them and laughed. "Crikey, Sammy, if you think this is competitive, you should see me and my bro when we have our speed shearing contests – you've never seen so many sheep trimmed so quickly."

Jimmy couldn't help liking the loud, confident tomboy. She lived in the Australian Outback and was an expert at tackling difficult terrain with her giant robotruck Monster. Jimmy liked Missy's sense of humour and the mad games she came up with.

"That wasn't in the rules!" Missy shouted now, a smile on her face.

"You made up the rules two minutes ago!" argued Chip. "Jimmy, whose side are you on?"

"Whoa, keep me out of it!" Jimmy laughed. "You'll have to fight it out yourselves."

Just then the door slid open and Horace Pelly walked in, his tray overloaded with food.

"Hey, Horace!" said Chip cheerily.

Horace ignored him, heading for a different table where he sat down with his back to the group.

Horace was the only robot racer Jimmy had known before the competition started, although he wouldn't exactly have said they were friends. In fact, Jimmy had mixed with the school show-off about as well as cornflakes went with pickled onions ... not very well at all.

Jimmy shook his head as he thought about life back in the little town of Smedingham. He wondered what his best friend Max was doing now, and if Max missed seeing him at all. Sometimes he wished that Max could be on the airship too. It would be great to show him round the workstations, the swimming pool and the games room on board.

Jimmy popped a slice of tomato in his mouth and looked over at Horace. He sighed. *"Treat others the way you'd want to be treated,"* was what Grandpa always said, and Jimmy knew that sitting on your own was no fun.

"Hey, Horace," he called over. "There's a space at our table if you want to eat with us."

Horace gave a snort of laughter and turned to

Jimmy with a sneer on his face.

"With you? No thanks!" he said. "I don't fraternize with the competition. And keep the noise down, will you? This place sounds like the zoo at feeding time."

Jimmy's face turned red. *I should have known he'd throw it back in my face*, he thought. He opened his mouth to talk to Princess Kako, but just at that moment a loud blare came from the other side of the room.

Horace had switched the television on, and the Robo TV theme tune sang out at full volume. Jimmy hadn't even known there was a TV in the canteen, but when he turned to look he saw that one of the large white walls was actually a giant electron plasma screen. He recognized the presenter immediately – it was Bet Bristle, an elderly but lively interviewer he had first met before the Rainforest Rampage race. Up on the massive TV, her usually dainty little nostrils were the size of dinner plates.

"Welcome to another edition of *Full Throttle*," she grinned, "the Robo TV show that lifts the bonnet of the Robot Races and takes a good look inside."

"I hope they don't look under Cabbie's bonnet,"

joked Jimmy. "Grandpa left his toolkit under there last week!"

"Shhh!" said Horace.

"We've got a great show for you this week!" said Bet Bristle. "So stay tuned!"

CHAPTER TWO
Scores on the Board

"It was a gamble for Lord Leadpipe to run a special version of his famous Robot Races Championship with kid competitors, but it seems to be paying off, as viewing figures around the world are growing and growing," Bet was saying from her TV studio. "The first race saw our drivers take on the Grand Canyon, and Princess Kako rocketed to first place with Lightning. The underdogs of the competition, Jimmy and Cabbie, surprised everyone by coming in second and performing this unexpected move..."

The TV cut to a video of the race and Jimmy recognized the manoeuvre they were about to show.

Missy and Monster were out in front with Jimmy and Cabbie in hot pursuit. A rocket launched from Cabbie's bonnet, transforming into a steep metal ramp which landed on the track ahead. The robot raced up it, sailing high into the sky before landing in front of Monster to complete the daring overtake. Jimmy's tummy turned over just watching it, just as it had when he was driving.

"Pfft!" said Horace. "What a fluke!"

"And Jimmy continued to impress when he flew into equal first place in the next race, down in the jungle," said Bet. The image switched to footage of Cabbie and Maximus racing neck and neck to the finish line, and then cut to him and Sammy jumping up and down in celebration. "Samir picked up his first winning place too, in the same race that saw *this* happen…" The screen now showed the lush hot jungle, and the muddy track which passed through what looked like a wide yellow lake – quicksand.

"Oh no," said Horace.

"Ooooh, yes!" said Missy.

The TV showed Horace racing side by side with Jimmy, both of them trying to edge into the lead.

Suddenly, Chip surged forward in Dug and unleashed a smoke bomb, hiding them all in a cloud of fog. Cabbie managed to take the lead, but Horace panicked and spun Zoom off the track, into the thick sludge of the quicksand below.

The rest of the gang knew that the smoke bomb had been payback for the previous stage when Horace and Zoom had tried to sabotage Chip's race.

"Ugh!" said Horace. "I can't believe they showed that!"

"And recently we saw an epic race across the frozen Arctic tundra…"

The screen flicked to a montage of the best bits of the race. It showed Zoom skidding across the ice, spinning out of control before regaining traction and powering away. Next, it showed Cabbie firing a grappling hook and pulling himself ashore after he'd become marooned on an ice floe.

"Brrr!" said Jimmy. "It makes me shiver just looking at that!"

They saw clips of Monster racing across the snow and Lightning transforming from a bike to a jet ski. Finally, the TV showed a sight that Jimmy hated to see – Horace crossing the finish line in first place.

"Yes! Get in!" shouted Horace.

Jimmy shook his head – the TV hadn't shown the part where Horace had put everyone in danger by using his boosters and almost causing an avalanche...

The screen flicked back to the studio, where Bet Bristle was grinning. "Well, that's our recap over and done with. Now, let's see who's in pole position, and whose chances have suffered a puncture!"

She turned to a screen next to her. "Samir Bahur currently sits at the foot of the leaderboard with twelve points." On the screen a picture of Sammy flashed up.

"A handy second-place finish in the last contest lifted Missy McGovern to fourteen points, while Princess Kako and Horace Pelly share third place with sixteen points."

Photos of Horace and Missy appeared above Sammy's on the screen, with their scores next to them.

"Chip Travers has shown plenty of consistency in getting to joint first place on eighteen points along with the surprise package of the championship – Jimmy Roberts. Jimmy's tally could have been increased further if it hadn't been for the heroics which led to his puncture at the North Pole."

"Hear, hear," shouted Missy over the sound of Bet's voice. "The rest of us should count ourselves lucky that he saved our backsides from that glacier. But don't think that means we're gonna take it easy on ya this time, Jimmy. I've never let anyone win in my life, and I ain't gonna start now."

"I wouldn't want it any other way," Jimmy said, smiling at Missy. He turned back to the TV.

"I'm Bet Bristle, and I'm sure you'll join me in wishing everyone the best of luck," the presenter was saying, "and you'll want to tune in tomorrow when we show live coverage of the next race ... wherever that may be!"

Zzzip. The screen went blank as the bell rang for the start of lessons.

"Ah, strewth! I'd hoped to get a clue where we're headed," Missy grumbled.

Still complaining, the racers tidied away their lunches, picking up the crumbs and shards of crisps lying around their table before walking through the airship to their next lesson.

As they passed through the main workshop Jimmy looked around for Grandpa. The workshop was a giant room built like a hangar in the centre of the ship. It was where all the teams worked on their racers between rounds of the competition.

Jimmy saw Grandpa at the other side of the workroom. He wasn't hard to miss – he was much older than the other technicians, with white hair and a droopy moustache. He was also dancing around his robot singing "Happy Days Are Here Again" and juggling with three spanners. Cabbie was providing backing vocals. Grandpa was the only one in the workshop who looked like he was having a good time. All the other mechanics and technicians were deadly serious, frowning over plans and blueprints and carefully upgrading their state-of-the-art robots.

Cabbie had been made from a clapped-out old taxi cab and a lot of scrap metal. He might not look as sleek and professional as the other robots, but Grandpa had been a genius when it came to programming the artificial intelligence that made the robot talk and think. Cabbie was one of the most intelligent robots to ever compete in the Races. In fact, it was sometimes a struggle to get Cabbie to be quiet!

Jimmy waved, and Grandpa caught sight of him and dropped his spanners with a clang. He waved back and shouted across the space, making the other crews look up.

"All right, Jimmy? I'm just having a tinker! Wait until you see what I've done with Cabbie. Pete and I have made a few adjustments that'll knock your socks off in the next race!"

Jimmy smiled back and gave Grandpa a thumbs-up. He couldn't wait to find out what new equipment he'd have for the next round, especially any ideas that Pete Webber had brought to the team. He was the world-class engineer behind Crusher – the robot driven by former Robot Races' champion and Jimmy's idol, Big Al. It had been sad to see Pete leave two days earlier, but he'd had to go and help Big Al at a Destruction Derby in Texas.

"Jimmy, Jimmy, when can we go out and race? I'm going to show the others a clean pair of tyres this time," hollered Cabbie across the cavernous room.

"Soon, Cabbie!," Jimmy shouted back with a smile. Just then Horace barged past him, knocking his shoulder. "Ha! I can't wait to see Scabbie race again either, Jimmy. I haven't had a good laugh in a while!" he said, snorting with laughter.

Arriving at the classroom, Jimmy took his place at the front of the class. He tried to ignore Horace's nasty comment and concentrate on the lesson.

Leadpipe's school was certainly a bit different from Jimmy's school in Smedingham. The rooms were equipped with the latest technology – a fully computerized whiteboard hung from the wall, and rising up from their desks came individual 3D holo-screens. The familiar Leadpipe Industries logo of a revolving 'L' floated in mid-air a few centimetres above Jimmy's desk. *But one thing was the same*, Jimmy thought as he felt a kick on the back of his chair and looked round to see Horace behind him. *I'm thousands of miles from home, but I still have to put up with Horace Pelly!*

"Oops, did I kick you?" Horace asked. Jimmy tried to ignore him and turned back to face the front. "Oops, did I do it again?" Horace said, kicking once more.

Horace stopped as the teacher came in. He was an

old man, thin and so frail that it looked like he could be blown over in a strong wind, but he held himself like a soldier, with a straight back and chin held high, even though he walked with a stick.

"Who's this old loon?" whispered Horace.

"Do sit down," said the teacher. "My name is Sir Rupert Huxley, and Lord Leadpipe has brought me on board to teach you survival skills."

"Blimey!" whispered Horace. "He doesn't look as though he'll survive the lesson!"

"Thank you, Mr Pelly," said Sir Rupert. "I may look ancient, but my hearing is tip-top, thank you very much."

Horace shut his mouth and sat back in his seat sulkily. *I think I'm going to like Sir Rupert!* Jimmy thought with a grin.

"I'm going to teach you how to cope when you find yourself in the most extreme environments on earth. You never know when you might find yourself in a tight spot without a safetybot in sight," Sir Rupert said with a knowing wink towards the racers.

Jimmy and the others nodded. There had been a close call in the last race when a glacier had almost crushed them all. There hadn't been anybody within 50 miles to help them, and the robots Lord Leadpipe had created to protect them from danger had malfunctioned in the cold weather.

"We already know all about that." Horace interrupted. "We've all just completed a race in the Arctic, after all."

Sir Rupert nodded. "True, true. I expect you utilized a lot of techniques that I will remind you of. I myself have trekked to the South Pole three times. I only meant to go twice, but I left my toothbrush behind once and had to go back for it," he said, a twinkle in his eye. The class laughed. "Negotiating a cold environment is a tricky thing. Snow and ice can be killers, but may also save your life by providing water and shelter. Antarctica is a particularly interesting place to visit, I think – did you know that it is the largest desert on earth?"

"Don't be ridiculous!" Horace interrupted rudely. "Everyone knows that deserts are hot and sandy."

"Pay attention, Master Pelly, and you might learn something *helpful*," Sir Rupert perched on his desk and pointed with his cane. "Actually, a desert is anywhere

where there isn't much water. In fact, deserts get less than twenty-five centimetres of rain each year."

"Oh yeah!" Missy said. "Antarctica is full of ice and snow, but there's no water because it's all frozen."

"Very good. Miss McGovern" said Sir Rupert. "You seem to know a bit about this subject."

Missy shrugged modestly. "I grew up in the Outback. Out there you have to know the land, or it could kill you."

Sir Rupert smiled and he seemed to come alive, a light coming on behind his eyes. "So true! If you learn one thing out of this lesson, it is to respect the land and your environment. Never underestimate it!"

"Are we supposed to go around hugging trees? Or kissing the ground we walk on?" Horace sniggered. But no one else seemed to see the funny side.

"Um, I think Sir Rupert means we should be careful," said Jimmy.

Horace shot him a scowl. "I know what he means, *Roberts*! My father says that land is there to be tamed. There's no problem that can't be solved by a chainsaw and a bucket of quick-drying concrete."

Sir Rupert looked at Horace with a slight smile on

his face. He had every reason to be angry – Horace was being quite rude now, his loud voice blocking out anyone else's questions. But Sir Rupert just leaned back and smiled.

"Enough discussion, I think. Time for a little practical demonstration."

He picked up his rucksack from under the desk. It looked heavy and worn, and Jimmy could imagine that it had been on every expedition the old man had ever taken part in. Sir Rupert placed it on the desk and opened the top.

"I've something in here which I think will interest you greatly," he said.

"Boring!" said Horace, leaning back in his chair, swinging precariously. "What is it, some old rocks? A branch to chew on when you get lost in your back garden?"

"Master Pelly, perhaps you would care to come up and help me out. The rest of you gather around," Sir Rupert continued.

Horace leaped up from his seat, keen to take any opportunity to show off. The rest of the racers approached carefully. They stood slightly back from the desk as the teacher rummaged in his bag.

"When I say I want you to respect the land around you, I—"

"Oh, let's get on with it!" said Horace. He barged forward and picked up the rucksack, turning it out onto the desk. The contents fell out, books and clothes scattering everywhere.

Sir Rupert tried to grab the rucksack, but Horace had it out of reach. Jimmy saw the alarm on the old man's face as a glass box tumbled out of the bag and onto the floor. It smashed into tiny pieces and Jimmy saw something crawl out of the shards of glass. It had eight black legs and two sharp claws. At the back of its hard body was a tail that curved above it, with a sharp sting at the end. Jimmy quickly realized what Horace had just released into their classroom.

A scorpion!

CHAPTER THREE
Scorpion Surprise!

Kako gave off a high-pitched scream as the scorpion scuttled under the classroom tables.

Chip jumped on his chair and started tucking his trousers into his socks. "Where'd it go? Where'd it go?" he asked anxiously.

"It's in the corner!" said Jimmy, who could see it heading for the door. "Actually, I think that it's more afraid of us than we are of it."

"I don't think so!" Horace shouted.

Sir Rupert sighed, and tried to continue with his lesson. "Come on, now, settle down," he said. No one paid him any attention. "Let's get back to the matter in hand, shall we?"

The scorpion scurried a different way, and the students all shrieked.

"*Stand still!*" said Sir Rupert with such force that everyone stopped panicking and stood to attention. "That's better," he continued in a quieter voice. "Now, if you'll all kindly take your seats, we shall continue."

They did exactly as they were told. They climbed down slowly from their chairs and sat down, except for Horace, who refused to budge from on top of his chair, his face red with fear. "Sting is a deathstalker scorpion," said Sir Rupert, ignoring Horace. "They usually live in the Sahara desert, where they feed on insects. The tail ends in a sharp spike, which contains a poison."

"You brought a deadly scorpion into our classroom? Are you mad?" squealed Horace.

"Now then, he's hardly deadly. A sting from this little fellow would not be enough to kill a full-grown adult," said Sir Rupert with his thin smile. He thought for a moment and the smile dropped. "Hmm. A child might be another matter, however..."

Horace moaned to himself and scrambled up on

top of his desk.

Sir Rupert carried on as if nothing had happened. "A fascinating area, the Sahara. Did you know that it gets less than twenty-five centimetres of rain each year?" he repeated himself. "You'd think that it is so dry that nothing can live there, but many animals do, such as scorpions, camels and goats. There is even a type of antelope that can go for a whole year without water."

"Get it out, get it out, get it out!" whimpered Horace as the scorpion crawled under his desk.

"All in good time," Sir Rupert replied with a withering look. "The desert itself is almost entirely composed of sand which forms in dunes. These are large hills or even mountains of sand made by the strong winds, known as the *sirocco*, that whip across the desert. The dunes can be very dangerous, especially when driving over them."

Horace was practically jumping up and down on the table now. "Please! Take it away!"

Missy rolled her eyes and stood up. "Keep your pants on. I'll get it."

She calmly grabbed her metal pencil case and

emptied it on the desk. Then she walked over to the scorpion and trapped it under the tin, as easily as if she was dealing with a fly. Carefully she took it over to Sir Rupert, who took the case with a warm smile. "Thank you, Missy. You weren't scared?"

"Nah," she said, sitting back down. "Not really. I've seen bigger. Once I woke up to find a forest scorpion on my pillow. Big as a dingo, that critter was!"

"Excellent! Everyone should take a leaf out of Miss McGovern's book. Keep calm, keep cool, and if possible keep away."

Horace jumped down from the desk. "You're insane! You'll never work again! Releasing a scorpion into a classroom? My father will hear of this!" he said, hurrying to the door.

"I don't know what Horace is complaining about – *he* smashed the glass," said Chip.

"Well, what's done is done," said Sir Rupert, packing Sting away in his rucksack. "We'll call it a day, I think. Good luck to everyone for the next race!"

"Wherever *that* might be," said Kako.

Sir Rupert smiled, and Jimmy saw the glint of mischievousness again. "Well, if you've been paying attention in this lesson, you should know everything you need to about the location of the race." Then he tapped the side of his nose as if to say, "*you didn't hear it from me.*"

Jimmy smiled and felt his heart pumping faster. He looked into the faces of each of the four remaining racers in the room and in a breathless whisper said, "I think I know where we're going."

At that moment they heard a *bing!* through the airship's speakers, followed by the robot co-ordinator Joshua Johnson's clear voice saying, "Ladies and gentlemen, we will be landing in approximately ten minutes. That's ten minutes."

Jimmy and the other racers burst out of the classroom like they'd just heard the starting pistol at the start of a sprint. Jimmy felt the slight turn of the airship, the floor tilting underneath him.

"Last one to the observation deck is a rusty wheel nut!" Missy yelled, and sped off down the corridor with a whoop. Jimmy and Sammy caught each other's eye and smiled, before charging off down the corridor after her.

The racers ran as fast as they could down the

length of the ship, passing Horace on their way to the observation deck, a room at the very bottom of the airship that was entirely made out of glass – even the floor!

Jimmy gasped when he saw the vast landscape below him. Looking down past his dirty trainers and through the transparent floor, he could see the huge yellowy-orange carpet of desert. His stomach lurched a little as he realized that there was just a piece of glass between him and a huge drop to the earth below.

"*Sugoi!*" said Kako, which Jimmy had learned meant "Awesome!" in Japanese.

"Woah!" said Chip, stepping out onto the deck.

"I knew it," Jimmy gasped. "We're racing across the Sahara!"

CHAPTER FOUR
Gadgets and Gizmos

Jimmy tore out of the observation deck and back into the corridor. *I've got to tell Grandpa about the location of the next race,* he thought. Cabbie would need to be adapted for the sandy terrain.

He ran to the workshop, where technicians and engineers were going crazy, running about and falling over each other in a mad panic to try and get their robots ready in time.

"Looks like someone's already told them about the desert!" Jimmy muttered to himself. He walked over to Grandpa, who was hopping and dancing around Cabbie like someone had dropped a lit firecracker down his trousers.

"You've heard, then?" said Jimmy, ducking out of the way as Grandpa whizzed past him carrying a giant antenna. Grandpa turned to smile at him, his moustache bobbing up and down excitedly.

"Of course I have! The word got around in seconds!" he beamed. "The Sahara desert! Just think of it, Jimmy!"

"We've just been down to the observation deck to take a look, Grandpa. It's so *big*!" Jimmy said. "It's massive! Vast! Enormous!"

"Brilliant!" said Cabbie, cheery as ever. "I love a bit of sand surfing. Bring it on!"

Grandpa continued rushing around Cabbie, making last-minute checks. Jimmy kept getting in the way, so Grandpa chucked a parcel at him. "Here, open this. Came this morning on the post plane."

Jimmy recognized the address label. "Great! It must be my new race suit. *That's Shallot!* promised me one ages ago." It was the first good thing that his rubbish sponsors had done for him. While all the others had cool sponsors like *Luke's Lasers* and *Robotron Rocket Boots*, the only people that had wanted to sponsor Jimmy and Cabbie when they started racing were a fruit and vegetable shop, *That's Shallot!*. Jimmy struggled to unwrap the large box, and wondered why it was so bulky. The jumpsuit he had wanted was made of flame-retardant, heat-reflective foil microfibres. It was super-shiny and extra lightweight, but the suit that eventually popped out of the box wasn't what he had been expecting.

"What the ... ?" he muttered, mystified.

"Try it on, then!" said Grandpa.

Jimmy pulled on the suit, which was large and made of plastic. It was completely brown, with some black stripes and a small tag that said 'pull here'. He tugged at the tag and a loud hissing sound came from somewhere inside the suit. It was expanding!

By now everyone in the workshop had heard the strange noise. They had stopped work and were looking at Jimmy in his strange new suit, which was inflating by the second. It stopped, leaving a perfectly round suit with his legs, arms and head poking out.

"It's ... it's ... an onion!" he said, baffled. The technicians around him gave a laugh and even Grandpa and Cabbie couldn't stop their giggles. Grandpa reached into the box and pulled out a strange leafy green helmet, which he placed on Jimmy's head. Jimmy wasn't impressed.

"Aw, come on Jimmy! It's nothing to cry about!" said one of Horace's NASA technicians through the laughter.

"He's not crying – that's the onion making his eyes water!" joked another.

Jimmy took off the suit, pulled out the stopper and chucked it into his locker in disgust. The onion deflated with a slow farting sound. "There's no way I'm wearing *that* on TV," he mumbled.

A few minutes later, they landed in the heart of the desert. Jimmy could feel the heat rising already as he made his way to the exit hatch with the rest of the racers and their teams. He was glad to be back in just his everyday clothes – an old grey T-shirt, shorts and tatty trainers – rather than that horrible, hot vegetable suit. *At this temperature, I'd have been a roasted onion!* he thought to himself as the gigantic hangar doors began to inch their way open.

"Everyone gather round!" Joshua Johnson, the robot co-ordinator yelled. "Lord Leadpipe has a special announcement to make."

"What does Loonpipe want now? Is it not enough that he steals us away from our homes—" Grandpa muttered.

And makes us live in the lap of luxury, thought Jimmy.

Jimmy knew Grandpa hated Lord Leadpipe. They had worked together as inventors when they were young men. But when Grandpa had invented the first-ever robot, his designs had been stolen and Leadpipe had set up his own robotics company. Lord Ludwick Leadpipe had gone on to become a multi-billionaire, while Grandpa had spent years as taxi driver, before he dusted off his workshop to make Cabbie for Jimmy.

They stepped through the exit hatch onto the ramp that took them down to the desert floor. Jimmy was hit by the dry desert heat as he moved out of the air-conditioned atmosphere of the airship. It struck the back of his throat, making him instantly thirsty.

Lord Leadpipe stood at the end of the ramp on a small stage that had been hastily set up. Somehow he was still wearing his usual formal suit and tie, even though Jimmy was roasting in just a T-shirt. As the racers came down the ramp, Leadpipe welcomed them all in his usual jovial manner.

"Come, come! Gather around! I trust you have had a good trip?"

"I've had worse!" Missy answered back.

"Good, good!" Lord Leadpipe waited until everyone was silent and a couple of Robo TV camerabots were hovering in front of him. He liked an audience, especially an audience of hundreds of millions, eagerly awaiting his every word. "Welcome, one and all, to the Sahara desert, among the harshest environments on Planet Earth! Tomorrow's race promises to begin one of the toughest events of your lives."

"Can't wait," whispered Missy.

"You will travel from this point across the sands to a finish line that we have set up on the other side of the desert. The eagle-eyed amongst you will have noticed a difference in this leg of the competition."

Horace surprised Jimmy by being the first to notice. "Where's the track?" he asked.

"Precisely, Mr Pelly!" yelled Lord Leadpipe. "This time there will be no track! Your robots will have to trek across the sands to the finish line at a beautiful little oasis I know of. In fact, it's where Lady Leadpipe and I had our honeymoon. The water is crystal clear and the palm trees are just lovely at this time of year—"

Joshua Jackson coughed and Lord Leadpipe seemed to remember they were all there.

"Anyway," he continued. "The finish line is nearly twelve hundred miles away, but this race there will be no pit stops *and* no communication with your pit teams!"

The assembled racers and teams murmured in surprise and panic.

"Your robots will have to be fully adapted to carry all the fuel they need. Our own robot teams will check over the vehicles and rewire the Cabcoms so you can only communicate with each other. One of the checkpoints will act as your overnight stop, but you will not be allowed to change anything on your robots while you are there."

Horace looked up at his dad, Hector Pelly. Hector looked exactly like his son, with perfectly aligned white teeth, a straight nose and glossy hair.

"This should be a piece of cake, Father. Zoom's

laser guidance system will work out the quickest route in no time!" he boasted.

"Ah! That reminds me," Lord Leadpipe overheard. "To make things a bit more interesting, our technicians will be removing any automated navigation systems."

"What?" said Horace and Mr Pelly in unison.

"All Global Positioning Systems, sat-nav, mapping software and laser-guidance systems will be removed before the race. Instead, competitors will follow a set of clues from checkpoint to checkpoint, which will then lead you to the finish. You'll be able to find the checkpoints by looking for the usual Leadpipe Industries' logo, and following the clues you're given. Each clue will provide you with a set of co-ordinates to the next checkpoint, and eventually lead you across the finish line at the other end of the desert."

"*What!*" exclaimed the Pellys again.

"What sort of race do you call that?" added Horace.

Jimmy grinned with delight and exchanged a look with Grandpa, who was looking a little smug. "I know what I call it," said Jimmy to Grandpa. "A treasure hunt!"

CHAPTER FIVE
The Starting Grid

Jimmy woke up to the sound of engines. But it wasn't the low hum of the airship's hyperdrive engines which he was used to, but the roar of petrol motors coming from the centre of the ship. With a burst of excitement, Jimmy remembered about the race. As he swung down from his bunk, he noticed Grandpa had already left the cabin they shared. Jimmy threw his clothes on and went down to the workshop to see what was happening.

As he walked through the doors, he was hit by a wall of noise. Teams of mechanics, engineers and technicians were shouting and stamping their feet as groups of Robot Races' officials swarmed all over the machines with spanners and screwdrivers.

"Morning, Jimmy," said Grandpa.

Jimmy went over to Cabbie's side to join him.

"Morning. What's going on?"

"They're taking out the navigation systems," Grandpa explained, handing Jimmy a cup of tea and a jam sandwich.

Jimmy looked over to the other side of the workshop where Horace was beside his robot, Zoom. He was in full tantrum mode.

"You won't get away with this! If you so much as scratch that robot I'll report you!" Horace complained.

A team of five technicians were around, inside, underneath and behind Zoom, fiddling with hardware. Every so often, they would extract a gadget from the robot and toss it in a heap outside the car.

Zoom didn't take kindly to this interference, and revved his engine menacingly. "*Error!*" he bleeped at them. "Unauthorized hardware removal!"

"Looks like we might be a while here," said Joshua Johnson, peering more closely at the masses of electronic equipment on Zoom's dashboard. He left the technicians to it and walked across to Jimmy.

"Our turn," said Grandpa cheerfully.

"Good morning, Mr Roberts," said Joshua. "I'll need to remove any navigation systems from Cabbie."

"Be my guest!" said Cabbie.

A white-coated man came across and sat in the driver's seat. Jimmy recognized him as Cyril, the same technician who had installed Cabbie's Cabcom. He looked around Cabbie for a second, frowned, then aimed his electric screwdriver at the one piece of gadgetry on the dashboard. He turned it on and it buzzed for a moment.

"Woo-hoo!" giggled Cabbie as his Cabcom was rewired and his radar screen went blank. "That tickles!"

Cyril stepped out and dropped a small microchip into Joshua's hand. With a curt nod he moved on to the next robot. The whole process had taken less than ten seconds.

Joshua peered into his hand at the tiny circuit Cyril had removed and frowned, unimpressed. "Hmm. I thought that would take longer," he said. He shrugged and smiled at them. "Oh well. Good luck for the race!"

Grandpa took his automatic tea-maker out of his toolkit and dispensed some thick brown liquid into his mug. "It should be an interesting one," he mused.

"I'll say!" chipped in Cabbie. "With Zoom and the others stripped of their navigation gadgets, we've got a level playing field!"

"Are you feeling lucky, Cabbie?" said Jimmy. "This could be our best race so far!" He patted Cabbie on the bonnet excitedly.

"Just you be careful, you two!" said Grandpa, sitting down and stirring his tea with a spanner. "I don't trust Leadpipe as far as I can throw him."

"Don't worry, Wilfred! I'll take care of Jimmy!" said Cabbie.

"And I'll take care of Cabbie," Jimmy grinned.

Grandpa smiled, but he still looked concerned. "OK," he said finally. "Now let me show you something new I added." He leaped over to Cabbie's dashboard.

"I want to show him! I want to show him!" said Cabbie like a little child.

"All right! Keep your roof on! Take it away."

Cabbie revved his engine excitedly. "Wilf's been

hard at work. He was up all last night making me ready for the sandy terrain. Just look at this!"

There was a *beep* from inside the cab, and Cabbie's bodywork started to whir and creak. Two sets of caterpillar tracks quickly wrapped themselves round Cabbie's tyres, making him look like a tank. They were perfect for the desert environment.

"Check me out!" said Cabbie in a fake American accent. "I look a whole lot like Dug!"

They all laughed.

"The tracks should keep you stable on the sand, and spread the weight of the car more evenly when you need to get up those slippery sand dunes," explained Grandpa.

"But what about fuel?" Jimmy asked after a moment. "Will Cabbie make it all the way?"

"I was just coming to that," replied Grandpa. "I was a bit stumped about how to get more petrol in without making Cabbie too heavy. But then I remembered what you and Cabbie did in the Grand Canyon. So that's when I fitted *this*." He pointed to a fat metal tube fixed to Cabbie's engine block.

"It's the sonic-booster Lord Leadpipe gave us back

in the Arctic!" Jimmy exclaimed.

"That's right. But I've programmed it for a slow release. Instead of giving you a burst of speed over a short distance, it'll help Cabbie go for an extra thousand miles. Clever, eh?"

"It's brilliant!" Jimmy said.

HOOOONNNNKKKK! In the workshop, a giant horn sounded.

"That's the five-minute signal." Grandpa looked at his watch. "Better get in, Jimmy lad, it's nearly race time."

"Here we go!" Jimmy said. He gave his grandpa a hug, took the battered old helmet from his outstretched hand and hopped inside Cabbie.

As they trundled slowly down the ramp to the starting line, Jimmy marvelled once more at the beautiful golden desert. He tore his eyes away from the curving dunes and shimmering heat to take in the grandstand, which had been erected overnight. Thousands of fans had come out in the hot sun to see the race. He saw waving flags and banners being bounced up and down, while the crowd chanted the names of their favourite racer.

"WE LOVE CHIP! WE LOVE CHIP!"

"KA-KO! KA-KO! KA-KO!"

"COME ON, JIMMY!"

Jimmy took his position at the starting line as safetybots buzzed around the track. Next to him, Horace sat in Zoom, with a large box now welded to his dashboard. Jimmy was about to complain that he had somehow re-installed his laser guidance system when he realized it was an air-conditioning unit to keep him cool. It must have been a gift from Horace's sponsor, *Gleam Toothpaste*, because the unit had the picture of a pearly white tooth on it.

As he looked about, Jimmy saw that most racers had been given something cool and useful from their sponsor. Chip had electronically tinted windows to keep out the desert sun from *Luke's Lasers*. Missy was quickly checking over her robot with the help of a flashy new tool kit provided by *Robotron Rocket Boots*, while Sammy was sporting a new extra-lightweight breathable racing suit – just like the one Jimmy had wanted.

Jimmy looked to his side at the gift from *his* sponsors – a giant carrier bag of fruit with the slogan, *'your easy way to your five a day!'* on the side. *Oh well*, he thought. *At least I won't starve in the desert.*

The technicians cleared the track, which meant that the race was about to begin. Jimmy looked back to the edge of the airship's ramp where Grandpa stood with other family members and crew. While the crowds were going wild around him, and the other parents hastily tried to shout extra instructions to their racers, Grandpa simply looked straight at Jimmy and gave a quiet thumbs-up.

Then Grandpa and the other crews were herded up the ramp and back into the airship, which would take them to the halfway point.

"Ready, Jimmy?" said Cabbie as the starting lights lit up.

"Of course!" said Jimmy. His nerves had now turned into excitement. When he heard the voice of the announcer lead the crowd into a countdown, he felt his fingertips start to tingle. His body rushed with adrenaline once more as the engines revved and roared.

Three! The crowd chanted.

His foot hovered over the accelerator.

Two!

Sand started to fly as the robots spun their wheels on the ground.

One!

"Here we go!" Jimmy shouted as the crowd around him went wild.

CHAPTER SIX
The First Clue

The noise reached a crescendo as the lights turned green and the robots around Jimmy lurched forward onto the sand. Some made it further than others. Monster's massive tyres made it easy going for her and Missy as they sped off across the sand. Jimmy felt a blast of air nearby as Maximus's air cushions inflated and the hovercraft slid forward.

Jimmy put his foot down on the accelerator. Sand sprayed out behind them, but Cabbie wasn't moving!

Out of the corner of his eye, he could see that Princess Kako was also having a disastrous start. After travelling about ten metres, Lightning hit a bump in the sand and Kako was thrown clean off her robot. She landed with a thud on the ground, but quickly shook herself off and climbed back onto Lightning, shouting angrily in Japanese. She hit a button on the bike and a small robotic arm extended from the bodywork. It reached over the front wheel and whizzed over the tyre faster than the eye could follow. It was spraying a thick coating of rubber onto the tyres, converting it from a thin racing tyre to a fat off-road one. It finished the front and moved onto the back, and Lightning soon had two chunky pieces of rubber underneath him. Kako was soon driving clumsily across the dunes.

"This is awful!" Jimmy exclaimed. "Cabbie, our normal tyres are useless, we're going to have to break out the caterpillar tracks early."

"Don't worry, Jimmy! I'll take care of it!" said Cabbie. There were two loud noises from underneath the robot – CLUNK! CLUNK! – followed by a clackety-clack, clackety-clack sound as the tracks appeared over the wheels and began to grip the soft sand.

The crowd ooohed and aaahed in appreciation.

"That's better!" said Cabbie, sounding a little smug. "Now let's move it!"

Jimmy felt better as they started to whip across the sand in pursuit of Missy and Sammy. They passed Horace and Zoom, who had sped off in a shower of sand, but now looked like they were struggling. As Jimmy passed them, Horace was yelling and banging the steering wheel, and Zoom's engine was making a horrible grinding noise.

The one person who didn't seem to be worrying about the terrain at all was Chip. His huge digger, Dug, had been built with this sort of surface in mind, and once he'd got moving he was soon eating up the ground on the leaders. The yellow giant overtook Sammy, and Jimmy did the same just moments later when Sammy and his hoverbot chose a longer route round one of the mountainous dunes.

Five minutes into the race and the race order had settled down.

"How are we doing?" asked Cabbie.

"OK, I think," said Jimmy with a shrug. "We're not first, but we're not last either. Sammy, Horace and Kako seem to be behind us."

"That leaves Missy with Monster and Chip with Dug in front of us. We'll soon catch them up," said

Cabbie positively.

"I'm glad Grandpa fitted those caterpillar tracks, otherwise we'd still be stuck on the start line," said Jimmy. "Now *that* would be embarrassing."

As they travelled forward, the first checkpoint came into view, a large pole with the spinning 'L' of the Leadpipe Industries logo. Jimmy could already see two robot racers – Dug and Monster – pulled up beside it. From the checkpoint hung six compasses and six maps made of delicate papyrus.

As he approached, Jimmy saw Dug's robotic arm reach out and gently pluck a map and compass off the pole. Dug dropped them into the cab, where Chip quickly studied them. Jimmy watched as Chip looked over the map, played with the compass for a second, and then sped off to the east.

Missy, meanwhile, had to jump down from her driver's seat and collect the items herself. By the time Missy had made it back up to her driver's seat in the tall monster truck, Jimmy was nearly alongside. Missy must have been worried about slipping into third place because she set off in hot pursuit of Chip without even glancing at the map.

Jimmy slid to a halt and pulled down the window. He grabbed a map and compass and stared at them for a few seconds. He had learned to read maps with Grandpa on one of their camping holidays and, although it had been a long time since he'd tried it, he soon noticed something.

At the top of the map were some co-ordinates, marked *Checkpoint 2*. Jimmy looked at them once more and turned the compass round in his hand.

"Come on, Jimmy!" said Cabbie. "Let's get a move on! Monster and Dug will be miles ahead of us at this rate!"

But Jimmy stayed silent. There was definitely something wrong. He double-checked the co-ordinates. Then he triple-checked them, just to be sure.

"Chip made a mistake," he said.

"Pardon?" Cabbie replied.

"I'm sure of it. He must have been in such a hurry to stay in first place that he got the bearings wrong on the compass," said Jimmy, checking the map for a fourth time. "He went *east*, but the co-ordinates point to the *west*."

"What about Missy?" said Cabbie.

"She just followed Chip," said Jimmy.

"Then what are we waiting for?" said Cabbie with glee in his electronic voice. "Let's burn rubber!"

Jimmy put the map down and pulled the steering wheel round to the west, and Cabbie's tyres spat sand into the air as he sped off in the right direction.

"Woo-hoo!" cried Cabbie. "That means we're in first place already! Not bad going, Jimmy, not bad at all."

"Thank Grandpa! He taught me to use a map years ago," Jimmy said, thinking back to the holidays he had spent trekking across the countryside in an anorak and walking boots. They had gone on long walks, using the sun and the stars to navigate their way through bogs and muddy fields, before falling down exhausted in their holey little tent. Grandpa had taught Jimmy the importance of double-checking his map references and it had certainly paid off. He reached for the Cabcom to tell Grandpa about it, but as he tapped the screen he saw only fuzzy static and remembered that he wasn't allowed to speak to him.

"We'll thank him tonight, when we get to the

overnight stop in first place!" said Cabbie. "He'll be watching us on TV anyway, and he'll know you took the right direction."

Jimmy knew he was right. He focused on the sand in front of him. "Come on, Cabbie, we've got a race to win. The sooner we finish this, the sooner we can see Grandpa." He put his foot down on the accelerator, and launched them up a dune. They reached the top and sailed into the air, Cabbie's wheels leaving the ground altogether.

"Yee-ha!" yelled Cabbie. "Winners' podium, here we come!"

CHAPTER SEVEN
Slippery Sand Dunes

Sand battered the windscreen and Cabbie's wipers were almost no use at all. But in his rear-view mirror Jimmy could now see two huge vehicles behind him. *Missy and Chip must have realized their mistake and turned round*, he thought.

Behind them, Jimmy could make out more specks on the horizon. He used the rear-view zoom function to magnify the image, so that he could make out Princess Kako and Horace. Horace had the map spread out across Zoom's windscreen, and a confused expression on his face.

"Ha!" laughed Jimmy. "No wonder Horace is

puzzled. He's got the map upside down!"

He reached out to the Cabcom and tapped the screen. Just because he couldn't contact Grandpa didn't mean he couldn't talk to the other racers. The screen fizzed and crackled, and soon Horace's smarmy face was staring back at him.

"Hi, Horace! Not so easy without NASA, is it?" he said. "Need any help?"

Horace didn't seem glad to see him. "Bog off, Roberts!" he shouted. "I'm surprised you made it this far. Cabbie's bonnet is so full of rusty holes that the sand must be passing through him like a sieve."

Horace's hand reached out and jabbed the screen hard, cutting off the connection between them.

"Someone's a bad loser!" sang Cabbie. Jimmy turned his attention back to the way ahead. They were right on target to find the next checkpoint, but Jimmy could see an obstacle ahead. A big one.

"Uh-oh," he said. Rising up above him was the biggest sand dune he had seen yet. As they hit the bottom of it, they slowed to a crawl. Cabbie's engine made a small screeching noise and Jimmy pressed a button to shift him into a lower gear. They began to climb the side of the dune, and the sand slipped from under them. "Come on Cabbie!" Jimmy muttered as they crept up the terrifyingly steep dune. If they stopped for a second they'd slip all the way down to the bottom! In his rear-view mirror he saw Dug and Monster closing the gap between them, followed by Lightning.

"Slow and steady, Jimmy!" said Cabbie. "Dunes like this can be dangerous. My sensors are telling me we don't have much grip. The sand keeps moving under the tyres..."

Jimmy nodded, but his attention was caught by Monster, who was charging up the slope. In a spray of fine sand she and Missy swished past Cabbie and regained the lead.

All of a sudden, the sand slipped underneath Monster and Jimmy saw a great section of sand fall and tumble down the slope towards him. It was like a giant yellow landslide carrying the monster truck with it. Jimmy saw a wave of sand come towards him in slow motion. He gasped in horror.

"Look out!" yelled Cabbie.

Jimmy jerked the steering wheel to the left to stop

himself from being crushed as Monster fell with the sand. But Cabbie wasn't in the clear yet. The blanket of sand swept over them, covering the bonnet and windscreen, pushing Cabbie back down the hill. The roar was deafening and the vibrations made Cabbie shudder.

Finally they slumped to a stop and the sand settled.

Jimmy checked himself over. He flexed his fingers and wiggled his toes and shook his head to clear the ringing in his ears.

"Cabbie? Are you OK?"

"I'm fine. But that was some trip!"

Jimmy couldn't see out of his windscreen to tell if they were upside down, facing front or back.

After a moment he faintly heard Missy shouting above him on the slope, "Monster! Hurry up and get us out of this mess!" A second later there was a deep roaring noise as Monster's huge engine burst back to life.

Jimmy had his own robot to worry about. He shifted into reverse and tried to move, but Cabbie was well and truly stuck.

"The sand on the bonnet is too heavy!" said Cabbie.

Jimmy couldn't even climb out to dig them clear with his hands. If a safetybot arrived now, he would be rescued – which meant he and Cabbie would be out of the race. Jimmy took a deep breath. He needed to stay calm. Grandpa always said that no one ever got themselves out of a mess by losing their heads. And then suddenly a thought hit him.

"Cabbie, open up the bonnet, and give it some welly!"

"Okey-dokey, Jimmy!"

Cabbie released the latch keeping the bonnet down, and the whole front section sprang up, sending a spray of sand everywhere. It did the trick, shoving off most of the sand on the front half of the car. He tried to reverse again, and it was easier this time. Finally Cabbie wiggled free from the sand and Jimmy looked around him.

Monster was heading back down the slope to help Kako, who'd also been caught in the landslide – Lightning was now buried deep in the sand, just one rear wheel exposed.

The princess sat up and removed her helmet. A pile of sand fell out. She shook her head rapidly to get the bits out of her sleek black hair.

"Crikey! You OK, Kako?" shouted Missy. "Here, we'll have you out of this in a jiffy."

Jimmy looked around the hot, bleak desert as Cabbie slammed his bonnet shut again. "Oh no, the others are getting away," he said. Down below, Chip, Horace and Sammy had veered left to go round the dune altogether. "I guess they saw what happened and thought they'd try a safer route," he added.

Jimmy turned back to see Missy do the right thing and hook a winch round Lightning's exposed wheel. She whistled to Monster, who slowly pulled the superbike from the desert.

"Sorry about that!" said Missy. "I guess Monster doesn't know her own weight!"

Missy and Jimmy stayed with Kako until she was safely back on Lightning. But once she had started her robobike up again, they all threw their racers into gear.

"You gonna be all right going up the dune?" asked Missy out of the high window of her monster truck.

"No, I think I will go around the hill this time. I will be faster on the flat ground," said Kako.

"Fair enough." Missy replied. "Happy travelling!"

"What do you think, Jimmy?" asked Cabbie. "Stay on the flat, or give the dune another go?"

Jimmy weighed up his options, staring up at the dune. "Let's go for it again. It should still be quicker this way."

Cabbie and Jimmy climbed carefully up the dune. Halfway up he glanced over to see Monster trundling alongside, so he hit the Cabcom.

"G'day, Jimmy! Glad to see you're taking the riskier route," said Missy, once the screen had cleared.

"I'm just keen to get ahead," replied Jimmy.

"Don't worry, I'll keep my distance this time." Missy grinned. "I'll try not to drag you down with me if Monster here causes another sandslide!"

They concentrated on speeding up the slope, but kept the com link open. Jimmy liked Missy, and she was always cheery and easy to talk to.

They reached the top of the dune, and Jimmy saw how high he was. He could see the desert spreading out below him, with Dug, Maximus and Zoom making their way toward the next checkpoint. If Jimmy squinted, he could just make out the revolving

'L' of the Leadpipe Industries logo, gleaming in the sunshine.

Monster appeared on the top of the dune, and Missy peered into the Cabcom's tiny camera. "What are ya waiting for, Jimmy? Last one to the bottom is a soppy koala!" She whooped with joy as she pushed Monster over the edge and began to streak down the dune.

Jimmy laughed. "You're on!" he shouted. "Hold onto your bonnet, Cabbie!"

"Okay-dokay!" said the robot. Jimmy edged them over the top of the dune and felt his stomach lurch as they skidded down the sand. "Geronimo!"

Jimmy turned out to be the soppy koala. As soon as they hit the bottom Missy fired her engine and they swept away in a cloud of sand. Jimmy sped along after her, trying to avoid the dust cloud she was leaving in her wake. He kept his foot hard to the floor as they both skidded up to the checkpoint.

Missy ground to a stop just centimetres from the checkpoint marker, her tyres sending a puff of sand high into the air. Jimmy hopped out to see what clues Lord Leadpipe had set for them. He removed his helmet just in time to see Sammy and Chip jogging back to their robots.

"See you at the overnight stop!" shouted Sammy.

Jimmy found four envelopes attached to the pole, each one with the name of a racer on it. He snatched up the one with JIMMY written on it and headed back towards Cabbie. As he climbed into the cockpit he ran a finger under the seal of the envelope and tore it open, eager to take a look inside. He pulled out another piece of ancient-looking papyrus. It was from Lord Leadpipe!

Dear Racers,

Congratulations on making it to the second checkpoint. You have done well to make it this far, but the hardest part still lies ahead. So here's a thought to help you on your way:

Chinese prophecy says that humans have been given two ears and one mouth for a very important reason, so that one can listen twice as much as one speaks. If you have been listening carefully to those wiser than you, perhaps you'll find these questions a doddle.

Yours,

Ludwick

Under the message were two multiple choice questions.

The largest desert on earth is…

a) the Sahara
b) the Kalahari
c) Antarctica

But as Jimmy glanced at this first question, his mind went completely blank…

CHAPTER EIGHT
Checkpoint Quiz

Next to Jimmy, Missy was already putting Monster into gear, setting off after Chip and Sammy without even looking inside her envelope.

"I don't like to waste time hanging about," she yelled over to him. "I'll do my thinking on the go!"

Next to each answer there was a numbers. A light bulb went off in Jimmy's head and he dashed back to his seat to get the papyrus map they had been given.

"The answers have map co-ordinates next to them," he said.

"So as long as we get both the right answers, we get the right co-ordinates, and we can find our way to the overnight rest stop?" asked Cabbie.

"Yep," said Jimmy. "Now, where have I heard the answer to this one?"

His thoughts wandered back to the classroom on the Leadpipe airship. He remembered Sir Rupert telling them all that the largest desert in the world was...

"Got it!" he said aloud. "It's Antarctica."

"Are you sure?"

"Absolutely! Sir Rupert was giving us the answers in that lesson all along." Jimmy traced his finger next to the answer and saw the number fifteen. He noted down the first co-ordinate.

Just then, he saw something out of the corner of his eye. It was Horace, sitting ten metres away on the bonnet of Zoom. He was staring at his piece of papyrus, but he didn't look like his normal, smooth self. He had taken off his helmet and his hair was sticking up in different directions like a radio mast. He was red in the face, but Jimmy didn't think it was all down to the desert heat. Jimmy saw the familiar frown that he recognized from sharing a class with Horace for years. He was trying to work out the clues, and if

Jimmy remembered correctly, Horace had been using his mouth much more than his ears in the classroom. Now he puzzled over the questions, grimacing like a gorilla with toothache.

"OK, hit me with the next one!" said Cabbie.

The paper was slippery in Jimmy's sweaty hands now, and he could feel a trickle of perspiration running down his back from the uncomfortable heat. But he forced himself to turn his attention back to the paper and concentrate on the second question:

How much rainfall, on average, do deserts get each year? Is it less than:

a) 25 centimetres
b) 250 centimetres
c) 2,500 centimetres

"Oooh, I'd say a?" guessed Cabbie. "No, b. Although, c could be right…"

Jimmy racked his brain for the answer. He remembered Sir Rupert talking about deserts. He'd said that deserts could contain ice and snow as well as sand, because a desert meant that there was very little water, not that it was hot. *And hadn't Sir Rupert said something about rain...?*

"Got it! It's less than twenty-five centimetres!" he said as the memory became clear in his head. "Definitely! Thank you, Sir Rupert!"

He quickly checked the co-ordinates matched to the answers he'd chosen and used them to take a reading on the map. Then he ran back around to Cabbie's driver's seat. He was about to pull the door shut when he heard the roar of an engine and Zoom surged forwards, skidding right in front of Cabbie. Jimmy's path was blocked.

Horace leaped out and grabbed Cabbie's door, keeping it open. "Not so fast, Jimmy!" said Horace.

Jimmy couldn't tell at first what was wrong. Something was different. Something he couldn't quite put his finger on. "Horace, are you *smiling*?" he said at last.

And he was. Horace was smiling from ear to ear, but not in his usual 'I'm better than you' way. This was more like an 'I want to be your friend' smile, and Jimmy didn't like it one bit.

"Hmm? Oh, don't be silly, Jimmy, old mate!" he said. "Hey, remember back in Smedingham how you used to let me look at your homework answers?"

"No," said Jimmy, trying to close the door. "I remember you stealing my school bag, ripping my homework out of the exercise book and handing it in as your own."

"All right, all right!" said Horace, the creepy smile dropping from his face. "I tried being nice. Now give me the co-ordinates!"

Jimmy laughed. He was almost glad to see Horace acting grumpy again – "friendly" hadn't suited him.

"Come on, Roberts!" Horace exploded. "I'll give you something. How about a turbo air-blaster? It's great for blowing sand out of your way. We could take it off Zoom now and strap it on Cabbie!"

"You'll do no such thing!" said Cabbie.

"All right – what about my robotic repair kit? It sits inside the bonnet, and then fixes a puncture in less than a second when you get one! If you'd had it in the last race you might not have come last."

"I might not have come last if you hadn't nearly caused an avalanche!" Jimmy said angrily.

"And we're using caterpillar tracks today, if you hadn't noticed!" snapped Cabbie.

"You haven't got anything that I want." Jimmy added. "Cabbie's perfect just how he is."

Horace scowled. "What? This piece of junk?"

"Charming!" said Cabbie.

"Horace, I'd rather have Grandpa's gadgets than your NASA stuff any day. Now, if you'll excuse us, we've got a race to run!"

Jimmy slammed the door shut and Horace looked madder than ever. In frustration he picked up a fistful of sand and flung it at Cabbie. Zoom revved menacingly.

"Fine!" Horace shouted. "Then I'll just *follow* you to the next checkpoint!"

Jimmy revved the engine. "Not if I can help it." He reversed quickly back, then shot past Zoom as fast as he could.

In his rear-view mirror he saw Horace scramble into Zoom and whizz after them. Jimmy had planned on that, and he quickly swerved behind a sand dune.

"Why are we stopping?" asked Cabbie.

Zoom went past them at speed, cruising along the

sand towards the horizon.

"Because," said Jimmy, smiling, "the overnight stop is *that* way." He pointed behind him. Zoom and Horace were going at top speed in the wrong direction!

The race was easy going for a while. It was mid-afternoon now and the sun was finally becoming less fierce. Jimmy was enjoying the drive – he didn't have to worry about Horace, and the terrain had flattened out so that he could almost drive at full speed.

"Robots in sight, Jimmy!" announced Cabbie. Jimmy leaned forward in his seat and could just make out the shimmering shapes of the other racers in the distance.

"It's about time we caught them up," said Jimmy.

Slowly but surely they drew level with them. Jimmy noticed that the desert was changing as he moved across it – the dunes here were even steeper than before, making them too treacherous to climb. This meant that all the robots were avoiding the sandy slopes, and were forced into the deep valleys between peaks. Jimmy and Cabbie closed right up behind the leaders, bobbing and weaving as the path between the dunes became narrower.

"Careful!" said Cabbie. "There won't be enough room for all of us!"

"Stop worrying!" said Jimmy. "We need to get ahead!"

"You always say that it's a *marathon*, not a *sprint*!" warned Cabbie. "We've got a way to go until the stop point. Take your time."

But Jimmy increased his speed instead and nudged his way between Dug and Maximus. Suddenly they were driving all in a line!

"This doesn't feel very safe," said Cabbie, as the two huge robots towered either side of them.

"It's fine, Cabbie," said Jimmy. "Stop being such a scaredy-bot."

"Have you forgotten the pile-up in the Arctic?" Cabbie worried.

"I know, I know, but we can't afford to come last again," Jimmy said. "We need to take a few chances. And it's not like Horace and Zoom are here to cause problems this time."

Missy gunned her engines and stretched away, sprinting forward to take the lead by a small distance. "See you at the rest stop, boys!" she gloated over the Cabcom.

A split-second later there was a sickening grinding noise. Jimmy whipped his head round to see what it was, and found the source immediately.

Maximus was going haywire! Something was definitely wrong with the hoverbot as it weaved from side to side across the sand, and Jimmy could see Sammy struggling with the controls. Then there was a thud as Maximus spun into Dug's path and Cabbie, hitting both the other racers hard.

Cabbie was sent careering up the treacherous bank of the dune!

"Watch out!" Cabbie yelled, and then everything turned upside down as he flipped over. Blood rushed to Jimmy's head and he could hear Cabbie yelling.

"Brace yourself!" Cabbie shouted.

Then everything turned black.

CHAPTER NINE
In The Dark

Jimmy was confused. Was he unconscious? Had he been knocked out by the collision?

Then a light appeared in front of him. He had heard about this on the TV. He would wake any moment in a hospital surrounded by doctors and nurses. He'd get better, but he'd lose the championship.

Then through his confusion he heard ... a beep. And the familiar sound of Cabbie's circuits rebooting filled his ears. What was going on?

"Cabbie?" he said.

"Super custard fish finger escapades," Cabbie's voice came out of the darkness.

"What?" Jimmy said woozily.

"The quick brown fox jumps over the lazy dog."

"Eh?"

"Daisy, Daisy, give me your answer dooooo..." Cabbie sang.

Jimmy was worried. "Cabbie! Are you all right?"

There were a few beeps, some more lights lit up on the dashboard and Cabbie was suddenly back to normal.

"Phew, sorry about that! I must've gone offline for a second. Just running through a few setup protocols! Are you OK?"

"I think so," said Jimmy. "Why is it so dark?"

"Oh, that's our air bubble," replied Cabbie.

"Our what?" Jimmy asked.

"Our air bubble. It's like an air bag but it wraps itself around my bodywork rather than inflating inside the car. Hold on a second, I'll deflate it."

There was a beep and a hiss, and several jets of air blew into the driver's seat from outside. Slowly, light came back inside the cab and Jimmy could see what had happened. They had been cocooned inside a giant rubber balloon!

"Pete and your grandpa fitted it before Pete left for Texas. Didn't they mention it?" said Cabbie.

Jimmy stared at the hissing rubber material outside.

"So when it looks like we're going to crash—"

"Woomph!" said Cabbie proudly. "Wilf calls it the bounce-buster!"

Jimmy could see the desert around him now. They had rolled to a stop about 20 metres away from Dug and Maximus.

"Give me a damage report, Cabbie," Jimmy said as the last of the air bubble disappeared back under the robot's chassis.

"Calculating..." said the robot with a beep and a buzz. "No damage whatsoever."

Jimmy was amazed. They had been bashed by a hovercraft, flung up the side of a sand dune and sent flying through the air – all without a scratch. He opened the door and hopped out, removing his helmet.

"I'd better see how Sammy and Chip are." He flicked on the Cabcom. "Hey, guys, are you OK?"

"I'm fine, Jimmy," Chip replied, his face appearing on the screen. "Dug here took a tumble and ended up on his side, but I was able to put him right again using the robotic arm."

"How about you, Sammy?" Jimmy asked.

"The screen in Cabbie's cockpit split into two so that Jimmy could see both of the other racers. "Yes, I am fine. Sorry about my mistake – this sand is proving tricky, no."

"You can say that again, pal," Chip replied.

"I said, *this sand is proving*—" Sammy began.

Jimmy laughed. "No, Sammy, it's just a turn of phrase. Chip heard you first time."

"Oh," Sammy muttered. "I will never understand the English language."

"All right, let's get this show back on the road, y'all," Chip said. "This race ain't gonna win itself and I've got me a trophy to claim. Catch me if you can!"

With a roar of their engines, the three racers shot off once again. Following the co-ordinates that he had worked out, Jimmy didn't find it too hard to locate the checkpoint.

As they crested a rise, the three of them gasped at the sight before them. They could see a town – the first sign of civilization they had seen since the airship had landed in the desert. It was another ten minutes of hard driving down to the town and there were just seconds between the three of them as they crossed the line.

Jimmy skidded to a stop and breathed a sigh of relief that they had made it in one piece. Then he got out of Cabbie's cockpit and took off his hot, sweaty helmet. Next to him, Chip and Sammy were doing the same.

"What took you so long?" said Missy, who was standing by Monster with a cold drink.

"Don't ask!" said the three boys together.

The overnight stop was in an abandoned old village perched on the edge of a great desert plain. It would have seemed like a spooky ghost town if it hadn't been for the amazing job the race officials had done of turning it into a luxury retreat for the racers. They had cordoned off an area for each pit crew next to the deserted buildings. On the other side of the village were a collection of huge North African Bedouin tents. Each team had their own tent, but inside it was more like a palace, with richly woven rugs, fluffy cushions and brightly-coloured bunks.

"Wow!" said Sammy, standing next to Jimmy. "This is a bit different to our overnight stay in the jungle. Remember that?"

Jimmy nodded. They had been stranded in the jungle with just a sleeping bag each, a pack of marshmallows to eat, a tarpaulin stretched over their heads and a robot who was scared of snakes. It had been fun.

At that moment Joshua Johnson appeared from one of the tents.

"Excellent race, everyone! I trust you are all OK after your little bumps and tumbles?" he said, full of energy. The four racers nodded. "Great! We've noted down the times you came in, and that's the order you'll leave in the morning. I suggest you get some food, fuel and plenty of sleep. Big day tomorrow!"

Jimmy slowly shuffled through the sand to where Grandpa was dusting down Cabbie. Grandpa broke off his work to give Jimmy a crushing bear hug.

"I missed you, lad!" he said. "I was so worried! I've been watching on the TV in the airship. Are you all right?"

"Can't ... breathe!" Jimmy gasped out.

"Hmm? Oh!" Grandpa released him from the tight hug.

"Thanks so much for installing that air bubble, Grandpa – it really saved us," said Jimmy.

"Don't thank me, thank Pete Webber! He had wanted to use that little gadget for years, but Crusher is just too big to have an all-over air bubble. He was happy to be able to use it on Cabbie!" Grandpa laughed, patting the robot on the bumper. "Quick thinking, Cabbie."

"It was nothing really," said Cabbie coolly. "Well, not for a perfect specimen of artificial intelligence like myself."

Grandpa wasn't allowed to make any tweaks to Cabbie during the overnight stop, so he busied himself by giving the robot a good wash while Jimmy sat down and tucked into a huge plate of food from the food tent. The robot was in good condition, and his caterpillar tracks had been working well.

As Jimmy rested, he could hear Missy in the compound next to them. She was in high spirits from her first-place finish. She was also giving her robot a clean, chatting jokily with Monster as she fussed around her happily.

"I dunno, Monster, what are we going to do with you? First place is all right, but when I say speed up, I want *real* speed!"

"Give over!" said the giant robot. "Call that driving? I've seen better reactions on a bullfrog."

"Oi! You're not too big to be melted down, ya know! I could turn ya into tin cans! I'd probably make more money from ya!"

Jimmy grinned at their good-natured banter. Chip was on the other side of him, his race team fussing over a tiny scratch on Dug's side while Chip discussed tactics with his dad.

"Good race today, son, but we need to keep an eye on that Australian girl. She's looking to take the title from us," said Mr Travers.

Chip shrugged. "She's a good racer, Pa. I'll see if I can distract her with a vegemite sandwich."

Sammy was having a similar conversation with his father, Omar Bahur.

"To be a winner, Samir, you must think like a winner!"

"Father, I have a better idea." Sammy replied.

"To be a winner, I must *eat* like a winner. I'm starving!"

Just then Princess Kako entered the town on Lightning. She looked like she'd had a tough time in the desert, and when she got off her robot, Missy and Jimmy came over to help her.

"Can I get you anything?" asked Missy.

"Two more wheels," said Kako, exhausted. "I'm thinking of turning Lightning into a jeep. It's the only way I'll do better tomorrow!"

Over twenty minutes after the princess, Jimmy heard the noise of another engine approaching as Horace pulled into the town.

"What time do you call this? You might as well have not taken part!" said Mr Pelly as Zoom's door opened and an angry-looking Horace stamped out, mumbling crossly about getting lost.

Father and son continued to bicker as they made their way towards the food tent. Jimmy couldn't hear what they were saying and was about to go off to his own tent when he saw something strange. Horace and Mr Pelly paused in the middle of their argument and shook hands. It was an odd gesture, Jimmy thought. As their hands parted, he saw something – a tiny glint of metal between their fingers.

Probably nothing, he thought. A ring, perhaps, reflecting in the sunlight? It could be perfectly innocent. *But I know Horace*, Jimmy thought. *And I bet he's up to something!*

CHAPTER TEN
Messages from Home

Jimmy and the other robot racers sat around a camp fire in the middle of the deserted town. It was dark, but they were well lit by the fire and the stars above. Jimmy had never seen anything like it. There were so many stars, and every one looked like a diamond, sparkling bright and white against the jet-black sky. The racers had all had a good meal, and while their teams fussed over the robots (all except Grandpa, who was playing chess with Cabbie), the competitors talked about what they expected from the next day.

"I expect it'll be pretty simple," said Chip with a wink. "I'm sure there won't be any surprises or panics."

The whole group burst out laughing. They had yet to run a race that went smoothly.

Just then Joshua Johnson came ambling over, the gold 'L' on his dark blazer gleaming in the firelight. He looked more like he was on his way to a king's banquet than preparing to spend the night round a camp fire in the middle of nowhere.

"I have a little surprise for you," said the robot co-ordinator with a broad smile. And without another word he produced a small tablet TV from his inside pocket and placed it carefully on an empty chair. He swiped his finger across the screen once, and all of a sudden an image flashed up in front of the racers.

"Hello, racers," Bet Bristle said from the screen. "It's been an exciting day, hasn't it? Congratulations to you all for making it this far."

The children shuffled a little closer so that they could hear what Bet was saying.

"As you are so far from home, Lord Leadpipe asked me to provide you each with a little treat. Something to remind you that your nearest and dearest are thinking of you during these testing times. Enjoy."

The screen changed suddenly and Jimmy found

himself looking at a busy town in a hot country. Shoppers, tourists and stallholders struggled to get into the picture and give a thumbs-up to the camera.

"It's Cairo," Sammy gasped.

Then the camera panned left and focused on a small, dumpy-looking woman with a nervous smile on her face.

"Mother!" said Sammy, louder this time.

"I have been amazed by the support that Samir has had from Egypt," said the woman on the screen. The name *Bahiti Bahur* appeared on the bottom right-hand corner. "I am very proud of him. We all believe he can be the next Robot Races' champion!"

The scene changed quickly. The TV now showed a place Jimmy knew well. It was his home town of Smedingham in England, but a richer, leafier part of town than he lived in. Bet appeared in a posh-looking front room with floral wallpaper and a lace doily on every surface. The microphone was pointed at an elegantly dressed middle-aged woman with rosy cheeks and a pearl necklace.

"We miss Horace ever so much. I worry about my little kootchy-face!" said the woman.

"Horace, is that your mother?" asked Princess Kako.

Horace didn't answer, but stared at the screen in horror.

"We love you, Horace!" the lady called. "Mummy sends kisses and cuddles!"

Horace's head fell forward onto the table in embarrassment. Just when Jimmy thought it couldn't get any worse for him, Mrs Pelly pulled out a stuffed toy which was dressed in a racing jumpsuit. "You forgot to take your lucky teddy! I'll give Jenson the Bear to Bet so she can pass him on when she next interviews you."

Bet smiled sweetly as she took the teddy.

"Aw, *Mum!*" shouted Horace at the screen as the other five tried to hide their smiles.

The image on the screen shifted to show Bet now in Japan. She stood in front of the Imperial Palace, interviewing a young man in a smart suit.

"Satoru!" shouted Kako. "That is my cousin!"

"Her Imperial Highness Princess Kako has truly brought honour to the people of Japan. The nation has been watching and sending messages of support.

Everyone is Kako-crazy! Look at the fan mail you are getting!"

Bet held up a handful of mail, and a few things the fans had made. There was a knitted toy of Kako, pictures of Lightning, and even a comic book with a cartoon Kako on the cover.

"People are making comics about you! That's so cool!" said Missy.

The TV changed to a small American town with bunting stretched across the main street and a sign which read: 'Chip Travers, Number One!' Below it stood what looked to Jimmy to be the entire town. There was a uniformed marching band, hordes of people, and even a squad of cheerleaders. Bet was stood next to a lady holding a flag with Chip's face on it.

"That's my mom!" said Chip.

"We're all rootin' for my boy Chip!" Mrs Travers said. "We believe he can win this thing and bring the trophy back to the good ol' U.S. of A!" Then the cheerleaders burst into song. "Chip and Dug, they're the best! They are gonna beat the rest!"

Chip laughed aloud as scene on the TV changed

to the Outback in Australia. It was a large farm, with abandoned cars and tractors strewn about.

"Ah, home sweet home!" said Missy.

A boy of about nineteen years of age stood in front of a barn, his arms folded across his chest. *That must be Missy's brother!* thought Jimmy. They looked exactly the same, right down to the way they dressed.

"All right, sis? You're doing a great job." He smiled.

"That's Scott, my brother. I haven't seen that no-good waste of space for weeks," said Missy.

"We know you can do it. Now hurry up and win this thing, the sheep miss ya!"

The TV changed again, and this time Jimmy knew it must be for him. But who would it be? He didn't have any brothers, sisters or cousins. His only family was Grandpa, and he was here with him. He watched anxiously as the camera panned over his school. Suddenly a familiar face came into view.

Max!

Jimmy grinned and leaned forward to hear what his best friend had to say.

Max seemed nervous in front of the cameras. "W-we're all really proud of Jimmy," he said, glancing at the camera shyly.

Bet smiled. "Were you and Jimmy always big fans of Robot Races, dear?" she said in her soothing voice.

"Yeah, we used to watch it together on my phone all the time. It wasn't that long ago that we were in this playground, shouting for Big Al to win," said Max.

Really? It seems like ages ago for me, thought Jimmy.

"We can't wait for you to win it, Jimmy, and bring the championship back to Smedingham!" Max said, holding up a big sign that read: 'GO, JIMMY!'

Then the TV went blank once again.

There was a long silence as they all thought about the family and friends they had seen on the tablet.

Then Horace got to his feet and dusted off sand from his expensive trousers. "Well, I hope you all have your runner-up speeches ready!" he said with a gloating grin. "Zoom and I will be hot on your heels tomorrow, and I'll bet my boots that we take first place!"

Jimmy rolled his eyes. But he couldn't stop thinking about what he had seen between Horace and Mr Pelly earlier. *If Horace is up to his old tricks again, I'm not going to let him get away with it*, he thought to himself determinedly.

"This time tomorrow, I'll be at the top of that podium and you lot will be eating my dust!" Horace continued.

"Horace, if I thought for a moment that you stood a chance of winning, it'd keep me awake all night," said Missy. "But I think you'll find—" She pretended to fall asleep on the spot and fell backwards into the sand, snoring loudly. The other racers laughed, and Horace shot Missy a scowl.

"You'll be laughing on the other side of your face, McGovern! My father says—"

"Scorpion! Behind you!" cried Sammy. Everyone turned to look where he was pointing, and Horace leaped to his feet like he'd had a firework lit under his bottom.

"What! Where? Kill it! Trap it! Somebody *do* something, quick!" Horace screamed.

Jimmy's heart jumped, but as he looked around the camp he spotted Sammy putting a hand over his mouth. Jimmy looked closer and saw that his friend was trying to hide a smile. His shoulders shook, his head bobbed and then he burst out laughing, unable to contain himself any more.

"He's just playing a prank," shouted Chip, who'd also noticed Sammy's expression.

"Ah, strewth, Sammy, that was a good one. You really had me goin' for a second," Missy giggled.

The others laughed too, and settled themselves back down. All except for Horace. He was still on his feet and his face was bright red in fury and embarrassment.

"Listen here, Bahur!" said Horace, almost spitting the name into the camp fire. "No one makes a fool out of me and gets away with it! You'll pay for this!"

And with that he stormed off into the darkness in the direction of his tent.

"Well, he sure had his pants in a twist, didn't he," Missy commented with a grin.

Soon after, everyone agreed it was time to get some sleep. They said their goodnights and walked away across the camp to their own beds. Sammy and Jimmy headed over to their Bedouin tents, still laughing about the scorpion.

"It's ... it's a ... SCORPION!" Sammy laughed, then

imitated Horace's high-pitched scream. "That was funny, yes? His face was – how do you say? A picture!"

Jimmy smiled too, but dropped it when Horace walked by, scowling at Sammy.

"Oops," said Sammy.

"Horace is angry with everyone, all the time. I wouldn't worry," said Jimmy, trying to reassure his friend. Secretly he thought that Sammy should be careful. He wouldn't put it past Horace to look for revenge once they were back out on the race track. And he'd already been acting suspiciously all evening.

I need to find out what he's up to, thought Jimmy. He said goodnight to Sammy, but instead of going into his own tent, where he could already hear Grandpa snoring, he crept towards Horace's tent. Slowly he moved nearer and nearer, until he could almost press his ear to the canvas.

"Receiving? Over," came a voice from inside. It had an electronic crackle to it.

"Affirmative, I am receiving, over," said another voice.

Jimmy inched quietly down the canvas and found a tiny hole in the tent wall that he could press his eye up against. Inside, Horace was sitting on his bed with a small glow of light coming from his hand. He raised his arm and spoke into his fist.

"Will this work?" he said.

"Of course it'll work!" said the electronic voice. It was Mr Pelly – he must be talking to Horace through the comms-device!

"Those stupid engineers won't think to look in your helmet. They only ever check inside Zoom for gadgets. This is foolproof!"

"It had better work!" said Horace. "I want to make those stupid kids eat their words. Make the directions clear, and we'll have first place wrapped up by this time tomorrow."

So that's what Mr Pelly had handed Horace! Jimmy realized. *They're going to use a communicator to keep in contact. Mr Pelly will be able to direct Horace, showing him the fastest way to the finish line!* Jimmy stepped back crossly…

Snap!

A twig under his foot broke in two.

"What was that?" said Horace from inside the tent.

Jimmy didn't wait to hear if Horace got up or came

out – he just turned on his heel and sprinted back to his own tent.

No wonder Horace is more confident, he thought as he ran across the cool sand. *His dad's going to help him navigate! What a cheat!*

CHAPTER ELEVEN
Lost in the Desert

WHOOP! WHOOP!

"YOUR ATTENTION, PLEASE! YOUR ATTENTION, PLEASE!"

Jimmy shot out of bed and fell onto the floor in a tangle of bed sheets as a siren continued to blare. He managed to stand up and peer out of the tent flaps at whatever was making the awful noise.

"THIS IS THE ROBOT RACES TEAM. TODAY'S RACE WILL BEGIN IN TEN MINUTES."

Jimmy blinked and saw where the loud-hailer voice was coming from. It was on an airship floating just 50 metres above them, with the words *RACE MARSHAL* down the side. Jimmy rubbed his head and yawned.

The voice continued: "MISSY MCGOVERN WILL LEAVE IN TEN MINUTES. CHIP, JIMMY AND SAMMY WILL LEAVE IN FIFTEEN MINUTES. PRINCESS KAKO'S START TIME IS FIVE MINUTES AFTER THAT AND HORACE PELLY WILL FOLLOW IN ANOTHER TWENTY MINUTES."

Missy walked casually past Jimmy's tent, on her way to the start line. She was already wearing her jumpsuit and helmet, ready to race.

"G'day, Jimmy!" she said. "Nice PJs!"

Jimmy looked down at his embarrassingly tatty Robot Races' pyjamas, which were covered with cartoon pictures of all the previous winners. He was definitely *not* ready to race. He ducked back inside the tent and kicked the leg of Grandpa's camp bed. The leg broke, causing the bed to collapse underneath him. Grandpa sat bolt upright with a jolt, looking sleepy and surprised.

"Hmm? *What? Who?*" he said, confused. "What was that for?"

"Twelve minutes," said Jimmy, tearing his suitcase apart to find his toothbrush.

"Twelve?" repeated Grandpa.

"Twelve! Until the race starts!"

Jimmy could tell that his grandpa was still half asleep. Grandpa scratched his head, white hair sticking out at all angles.

"Twelve?"

"It's *eleven* minutes now!" shouted Jimmy. "We need to get Cabbie ready!"

"Tea," Grandpa said, springing to life all of a sudden. "I need tea." And he dashed out of the tent, leaving Jimmy to climb into his racing gear.

High above them, the race marshal started a new announcement.

"RACERS READY! THE CO-ORDINATES FOR THE FIRST CHECKPOINT TODAY ARE 18, 42…"

Jimmy tried to memorize them as he hopped about the tent. He just had time to raid the fridge, which contained a new selection of disgusting breakfast creations from *That's Shallot!*

"Let's see," he muttered. "Will it be sprout croissants? Or cabbage flakes? No. Maybe a celery Danish pastry?"

He chose the carrot juice with a courgette yogurt,

as it didn't require any chewing so he could simply pour it down his throat as he went. He burst out of the tent with his helmet under his arm and ran to Cabbie, just in time to see Missy and Monster surge out of the abandoned town. They disappeared into the sand dunes.

Grandpa was waiting by Cabbie, holding out a flask of tea and a breakfast jam sandwich.

"Come on Jimmy, lad!" he grinned.

But Jimmy had suddenly remembered something – *Horace*.

In the morning rush he'd completely forgotten about the conversation he'd overheard the night before. Jimmy had planned to confront Horace that morning and force him to hand over the communication device, or else Jimmy would go to the race stewards. But now Jimmy was minutes away from missing his start time. He didn't know what to do.

"Come on, Jimmy, hop in," Cabbie yelled to him. "We don't have all day."

"Something wrong, lad?" Grandpa asked as Jimmy climbed into his seat.

Jimmy shook his head. It was too late now – he'd

just have to concentrate on his own race.

Anyway, he thought. *Horace is starting more than half an hour after Missy. He doesn't stand a chance of winning.*

"Good luck!" Grandpa bellowed. Just as he was shutting Cabbie's door, Jimmy heard a growl of anger.

"No, no, no! This can't be happening!" Sammy was rooting around inside the cab of Maximus, throwing out pieces of paper and rubbish.

"What's up, Sammy?" called Chip from the cab of Dug.

"I've lost my map and compass! I had them here yesterday but they are not here now. I cannot find the way without them, yes?"

Sammy ducked back inside the cab while his father shouted at a race official to do something.

This had the mark of a Horace Pelly trick all over it, Jimmy thought. He opened his mouth to tell Sammy what he suspected, but just then there was another *whoop! whoop!* followed by Joshua Johnson's echoing voice on the loud-hailer.

"Gentlemen, ten-second warning," he boomed. "Start your engines!"

Dug's powerful engine roared to life and Jimmy had no choice but to hit the ignition button on Cabbie.

"Even if I'm right, I don't have any proof that Horace stole that map and compass," Jimmy muttered to himself.

Then Dug's lights turned to green and Dug was off in a cloud of sand.

Jimmy put Cabbie into first gear and waited for his own red light to change. His foot hovered over the gas pedal for a second, and then the light changed to green and he slammed his heel to the floor. The caterpillar tracks whirred, Cabbie's engine roared and with a whoop of excitement, Jimmy sped out of the abandoned town.

Chip and Jimmy both set a terrific pace over the first few miles, and very quickly they'd left the camp far behind. Looking in his rear-view mirror Jimmy hoped to see a puff of sand or a glint of rotor blades that would be a tell-tale sign that Sammy was underway behind them. But he saw nothing.

Soon the desert terrain changed again. It became hillier and Jimmy found it hard to drive. Cabbie seemed to be enjoying the ride, though, tearing up and down sand dunes. They would crawl up to the top and free-wheel down the other side at top speed.

It wasn't long before Chip and Jimmy caught up with Missy, and the three of them ploughed on together towards the first checkpoint of the day.

"Cabbie, engage cruise control," said Jimmy. He wanted to look at the map briefly, so Cabbie took control for a few moments. Jimmy had a sneaking suspicion that something was wrong. They had been driving for ages but there was still no sign of the checkpoint, and what was more worrying was that no one else seemed to be following them. He put down the map and took control again, but tapped at the Cabcom screen. He linked to Monster and Dug, and Missy and Chip's faces popped up on the screen.

"I think something's gone wrong," Jimmy said. "We should have reached the co-ordinates by now. Do you think we've taken a wrong turning?"

Missy nodded, and they all agreed to pull over. They stopped where they were, on the brow of a large sand dune. As they got out of their racers, Jimmy could see the desert stretching out around them.

"Have either of you got a croc's clue what's going

on?" said Missy. The boys shook their heads. "I don't know where I could have gone wrong! I haven't misread a map since I was five years old!" she added.

"According to my calculations, we should be *here*," said Chip, pointing to his map. Jimmy and Missy nodded. "Which means there should be a small outcrop of rocks over *there*." He pointed to where he imagined it should be, but there was nothing there except mile upon mile of sand. Jimmy stared out at the barren yellow landscape bathed in the light from the hot, hot sun.

Suddenly he was hit by a sinking feeling in his gut, and he looked down at his compass.

"Oh dear," he said. "We've gone very, very wrong, and I think I know why…"

CHAPTER TWELVE
Back on Track

Jimmy got his friends to show him their compasses, and it only confirmed what he thought had happened. He began to explain.

"The sun rises in the east and sets in the west, yes? As it's midday, the sun should be over there, to the south..." He showed his compass. "But *this* says the sun is in the north."

"Which is impossible!" said Chip.

"So we've all got dud compasses?" said Missy. She threw hers down on the ground and shouted loudly, "How?"

Chip and Jimmy glanced at each other again.

"Horace," they said together.

"You can reverse a compass with a magnet. He must have done it last night," Chip added.

Missy kicked at the sand. "I'm gonna kill him! I'm gonna wipe that smug smile off his smarmy cheating face!" she said, burning with anger.

"Why didn't I notice this earlier?" Jimmy said in frustration. "We could be 100 miles in the wrong direction by now. And we're completely lost!"

This seemed to focus Missy, and she turned her attention to the map. "We're going to finish," she said grimly. "And then I'm going to get Horace. That boy is a dead dingo! All we've got to do is head back the way we came, which means reading the compass wrong," she continued. "Whatever it says to do, we do the opposite."

"That sounds confusing," said Chip. "If we keep the sun on our left, we'll know we're heading west. Then we can work out where to go from the landmarks on the map."

The two began to squabble over the best way to get to the finish line.

"Get a grip," yelled Missy. "We'll never make it if

we follow *your* plan."

"Oh, and *your* idea is so much better?" shouted Chip, getting angry.

"Well, it sure as kangaroo's dressing gown is better than—"

"Enough!" roared Jimmy. He even surprised himself with the force of his voice. Then in a quieter tone he continued, "we won't get anywhere if we stand around and bicker all day. We have to get back on track and we have to do it fast, because I'm not letting another Horace Pelly stunt put me in last place again. I've had enough of him cheating his way onto the podium."

"Ooh, somebody's got a bee in their bonnet," whispered Missy to Chip, but they were both grinning at Jimmy.

"Right," Jimmy said, ignoring the look on their faces. "We're going to follow *both* of your plans. Missy, you navigate your way with a map and compass. Chip, you use the sun to get us back. If we drive side by side, I'll notice if one of you starts to drift off at a different direction to the other, and I'll call for us to pull over. We can work out where we're going from there. OK?"

"OK," Chip agreed. "We work together now, but as soon as we're back on track, it's back to a race and you won't see me for dust!"

With a nod of agreement he and Missy hopped back in their racers. Jimmy fired up Cabbie's engine then threw him into a smart 180-degree turn and hurtled back the way they had come.

"Well, this is another fine mess Horace has got us into," said Cabbie. "I guess we can kiss goodbye to our place on the leaderboard."

For a few minutes they were silent. Jimmy was sweating now, the tiny fan that Grandpa had taped to the dashboard not making a shred of difference to the heat in the cab. Jimmy glanced at the clock and was reminded of the old saying: *'Only mad dogs and Englishmen go out in the midday sun.'* He understood that now – the sun was so high and harsh at this time of day that it was making the controls in the cab too hot to handle, and Jimmy was becoming seriously thirsty. He suddenly remembered that he had left all his bottles of water in the tent in the rush to make the start line.

Stupid, he thought. *That's exactly what Sir Rupert would tell you not to do!*

To top it all, there was a strange smell coming from somewhere...

"Oh no!" said Jimmy. "I left the fruit and vegetables from *That's Shallot!* in the boot! They must be cooking in the heat!"

"Urgh!" said Cabbie. "I wondered why my sensors were picking up the smell of warm cabbage!"

The stench was soon overwhelming, but Jimmy didn't want to lose time by stopping to open the boot. "Emergency measures!" shouted Cabbie. The boot flipped up and a coiled spring inside released, flinging the rotten vegetables out of the back of the taxi. Behind him Cabbie left a trail of hot, stinky cabbage, putrid pumpkin and festering cauliflowers. Jimmy felt Cabbie shudder with disgust.

"Would you *leek* at that," Jimmy joked. "You're like a mobile compost heap, Cabbie."

"Yuck! When this is all over I demand a full valet and car wash!" Cabbie complained. "I've got sand in my alloy wheels, filth in my windscreen wipers, and now I've got beetroot juice in my boot!"

Jimmy couldn't help laughing. Now the smell had cleared, the mention of food was making him hungry. "I could do with a snack," he said. "And a drink!"

"Hmm, well we can't have you going hungry, can we?" said Cabbie. "Flick that little switch on your arm rest."

Jimmy found the switch and pressed it. Out of the passenger seat rose a small fridge.

"I've been saving this, but now is as good a time as any," said Cabbie.

The door popped open, and a cool blast of air blew into the cab. It felt heavenly! Inside was an ice-cold bottle of water.

"Wow!" said Jimmy. "This is the best! Thanks, Cabbie!"

"Wilf wanted to make sure you didn't get stranded without any refreshments," Cabbie said.

Jimmy looked in the fridge and pulled out a box. "Why are there cones in here?"

Cabbie laughed. "It's a treat for you! There's only one food that comes on cones!"

"Ice cream!" Jimmy grinned in delight.

CHAPTER THIRTEEN
Speeding Across the Sand

Jimmy held a cone under a nozzle and out came a long white thread of vanilla ice cream, followed by a squirt of chocolate sauce and a sprinkle of hundreds and thousands.

"Amazing!" said Jimmy. "This is Grandpa's best invention yet!"

"Hey!" grumbled Cabbie good-naturedly.

Jimmy tucked in. The ice cream had started to melt already and he had to act quickly to catch the dribbles as they trickled down his arm. It was the best thing he'd ever eaten in his whole life! In twenty seconds flat he'd gobbled the whole thing and was wiping his sticky fingers on his jeans.

Grinning, he tapped the Cabcom and Chip's and Missy's faces popped up. "Snack time!" Jimmy sang. "Chip, can you get Dug's robotic arm over to my window?"

"Sure thing!" the American replied.

Jimmy didn't want to be greedy, so he prepared two more cones for his friends. When they were ready he wound down his window and passed them out to the giant metal claw that was waiting there. Jimmy was amazed to see the hulking piece of machinery delicately grasp the two ice-cream cones and pass one to Missy in Monster's driving seat, and one to Chip. All this while driving at high speed across one of the most dangerous deserts on earth!

"Cheers, Jimmy!" said Missy, with ice cream around her mouth. "That really hit the spot. I feel happier than a possum in a pouch."

"That was great." Chip agreed. "But I'd feel even happier if y'all knew where we were going."

Suddenly Cabbie's controls beeped and whistled in a way that told Jimmy he was having an idea. "Of course! Jimmy, switch to cruise control. I need you to press the flashing button on the dashboard."

"Um, OK," said Jimmy. He reached out and touched the button. It was one he hadn't seen before, a flashing purple 'P'.

"Up periscope!" shouted Cabbie as a long, telescopic pole shot out of the top of the roof and stretched up into the air for ten metres. On the end was a camera lens which pointed out at a right angle. It was a fully working periscope, just like in a submarine! A viewing pod dropped from Cabbie's roof and Jimmy pressed his eye to it. He immediately got a bird's-eye view of the desert below, and if he turned his head, the camera lens moved too, giving him a 360-degrees view.

"Your grandpa installed it before the race started. He took out the windscreen zoom feature and replaced it with this. I guess he thought that a zoom is no use if you're facing a wall of sand all day. Press the button on the handle."

Jimmy did as he was told, and the image in the viewing pod zoomed in. This meant that he could see all across the desert, and pick out details on the horizon.

"This is brilliant!" Jimmy put his hand out of the window and waved, hoping the camerabots would show it on TV so Grandpa would see. "Thanks, Grandpa!"

"Ahem," coughed Cabbie.

"Oh yeah, and thanks, Cabbie!"

Cabbie continued to keep up with Chip and Missy while Jimmy searched the desert with his periscope. It was so much easier to see where they were going. He could see the old town they had left, the outcrop of rock that Chip had mentioned on the map, and...

"Trees!" he shouted. "I can see trees!" He zoomed in closer and he could definitely make out a bunch of trees in the east, miles and miles away. He tapped the Cabcom and told the others.

"Amazing!" said Chip. "But what are they doing in the desert?"

"Don't be a drongo!" said Missy excitedly. "If there are trees there must be water! It's the oasis Lord Leadpipe told us about. Jimmy, you found the finish line!"

The racers whooped and hollered in delight. They had missed the checkpoint completely, but it didn't matter. The rules said that they had to get from the start line to the finish line using their own navigation, and this meant that they were all still in with a chance. Jimmy retracted the periscope and took control of Cabbie once more, turning the taxi towards the trees in the far distance.

"We can do this, Cabbie!" said Jimmy confidently. "We could finish the race with our head held high!"

"That's the spirit!" cried Cabbie. "Yee-haa! Team Jimmy, on the road again!"

The three robots climbed to the top of a sand dune and Jimmy could see in the distance the unmistakable plume of dust and sand coming from Lightning, and the silhouette of a hovercraft – it was Maximus.

"Sammy must have found a map," Jimmy yelled into the Cabcom, feeling happy that his friend was still in the race. "And, look! He's heading towards the finish— Oh, no. Is that Zoom ahead of him?" Jimmy's heart sank. He could hear a crunching sound coming from somewhere, and could have sworn that it was Missy grinding her teeth.

The three of them raced across the sand towards the oasis. Jimmy knew they'd all be going flat out for the win from here on in. Horace, Kako and Sammy were dead ahead of them, kicking up clouds of dust.

Through the periscope, Jimmy could see the crowds gathered around the finish line. The trees looked tall and green, set around a natural watering hole. Just behind the lake were marquees and Bedouin tents, with giant screens hung between cacti and palm trees, for the crowd to watch the race on.

"We're making great time, Jimmy!" said Cabbie.

"Good," Jimmy replied. "Because I want to make sure we beat Horace!"

"But he's miles in front!" said Cabbie.

Jimmy shook his head and pressed his foot hard on the accelerator. "We're faster than Zoom on this sand. He's cheated us all out of points once – we can't let it happen again!"

Jimmy chased after Missy, whizzing through the sand, Chip following after him. They sped down a slope and they were soon back on track, just a few metres behind Sammy and Princess Kako!

Poor Princess Kako looked tired, as though she might give up at any second. Lightning's two fat tyres still didn't make great desert wheels, and the sun was beating down on her exposed back, making her racing suit steam. Missy and Jimmy passed her easily, closely followed by Chip.

"Almost there!" Jimmy shouted encouragingly as they drove by.

Kako shook her head, and Jimmy could tell she was running out of energy. There was no way she was going to win this race now. It almost looked like she was driving through treacle. Every metre travelled seemed like a huge effort.

All the other robots were gunning for the finish line, jostling for position. Behind Cabbie, Chip and Dug began to lag behind in the difficult conditions.

But Cabbie was having his own problems...

"Engine reaching maximum temperature!" the robot shouted. Jimmy gasped as he saw steam rising from his bonnet. He frantically looked around at the masses of buttons in front of him, but he couldn't see any other engine-cooling gadgets.

"Do something!" cried Cabbie. "Or the engine might melt!"

"Melt?" The word struck Jimmy and he had an idea. "Cabbie – can you use the ice-cream machine to cool down your engine?"

"Great idea, Jimmy!" A grinding sound came from Cabbie's engine and then he beeped happily. "Press the ice-cream button, Jimmy," he called.

Jimmy hit the button, and gallons of ice cream went glugging under the bonnet with a satisfying hiss, cooling the engine down quickly.

"Ah! That's better!" sighed Cabbie. "Ooh, and raspberry ripple flavour? My favourite!"

"Come on, Cabbie!" called Jimmy. "We can make this! Together!"

"I'm trying, Jimmy," said Cabbie, straining. "But it's just too far. Unless…"

"What?"

"There *is* a shorter route."

As Cabbie said it, Jimmy saw the giant sand dune that rose up to their right.

"What do you think, Jimmy? It's all or nothing up that way…"

Jimmy hesitated for just a second. Twice they'd ended up in trouble during this race because they'd taken risks. Then he pictured Horace's sneering face mocking him for coming last. There was no way he was going to give up on the win when there was a chance of beating that cheater.

"Let's do it!" he shouted, and turned Cabbie sharply to the right.

Zoom took the low path around the dune and the rest of the robots followed. All except Cabbie, who roared up the dune away from the others...

Sand started to slip and slide under his tracks. Jimmy concentrated on steering while Cabbie's engine creaked and groaned as he applied more and more power to get himself up the mountainous slope. Jimmy hit the windscreen wipers as sand streamed across the glass, making it tricky to see. They were nearing the top of the dune now, the wind battering Cabbie.

Jimmy kept encouraging Cabbie as they reached the top of the dune. "Not far now, buddy! After this last bit, it's all downhill."

Looking down, Jimmy could see Zoom and Missy racing ahead, inching closer and closer to the finish line. Jimmy shook his head, suddenly feeling like he'd made a massive mistake. They were still so far from the finish and they'd used up gallons of fuel pushing themselves up a massive sand dune. "We'll have to go down the dune at full speed," he said. "Are you ready?"

"Actually, Jimmy," said Cabbie with mischief in his voice, "I've got a better idea..."

CHAPTER FOURTEEN
Finish Line!

Jimmy frowned as the dashboard buttons flashed and bleeped. He felt a clang and a jolt as something moved underneath him. He checked his seat belt and gripped the steering wheel.

"Cabbie, what are you up to?" he shouted. The din got louder as the whole chassis underneath him shook.

"Have you ever been skiing, Jimmy?" Cabbie replied. It was only then that Jimmy worked it out. Underneath the robot, the caterpillar tracks had transformed into smooth sheets, with no grip at all. They would be useless for climbing up sand dunes ...

but for sliding down them—

"Cabbie, we've got skis!" yelled Jimmy.

"Yep! So hold onto your hat, my friend, this is going to be one heck of a ride!"

"Woooo-hoooo!" they both screamed as they whipped down the steep slope. Jimmy could barely see where they were going as the desert around him flew past in a blur, but as he had no way of steering, he guessed it didn't matter. If he was going to hit something, there was no way he could stop.

They approached the bottom of the dune and Jimmy saw two racers in front – Missy and Horace. They were just a few centimetres apart, each of them eager for that first place title. They were pushing their robots to the limit, and Jimmy felt the heat from their engines as he reached the bottom of the sand dune, a cloud of sand following him. They were driving as hard as they could, but Jimmy had built up enough speed from skiing down the sand dune that he was catching them up. For a few moments he felt he could do it. He could see Zoom's back bumper, and he urged Cabbie on. He was desperate to beat Horace!

He held his breath as they got closer and closer to

the finish. Cabbie was sliding across the sand at an impressive rate, and Jimmy crossed his fingers.

Time seemed to slow in those last few seconds of the race...

He felt the burst of cheers and applause from the crowd...

He heard the squeal of Zoom's tyres...

He felt the heat of Monster's massive engine...

He just needed a few more metres ... had the finish line come too soon?

They whizzed over the finish line in a blur.

Jimmy hit a button and Cabbie skidded to a stop in the shadow of the great grandstand. He jumped out and looked up pleadingly at the scoreboard.

"Come on, hurry up," he grumbled as the screen remained blank.

Then the results popped up on the screen:

1ST PLACE: MISSY AND MONSTER
2ND PLACE: JIMMY AND CABBIE
3RD PLACE: HORACE AND ZOOM

A rush of energy coursed through Jimmy like

somebody had given him a shot of electricity.

"We did it, Cabbie! We beat Horace!"

But he couldn't hear the robot's reply over the screaming of the crowd. There were banners with his face on and thousands of people cheering for him. He waved his arms high above his head and then pumped his fists in excitement.

Through the racket of the screaming fans, Jimmy heard the unmistakable sound of Dug's diesel engines crossing the line. He turned to see the tired but happy face of Chip waving from his cab. He got out and his name popped up in fourth place at the leaderboard. Jimmy gave him a thumbs-up, and he looked to see who would come in next.

Next was Sammy. Maximus was jumping across the finish line, the rear propellers of the hovercraft full of sand and barely turning.

Moments later, a miserable Princess Kako stumbled into the finishing paddock on Lightning. The poor robot, who normally looked like a futuristic superbike, now seemed more like a rusty old tin can on wheels.

Lightning mumbled something as he passed. Jimmy didn't speak any Japanese, but he would bet that it meant, *"get me out of here!"* Kako looked ready to drop, her pristine silver jumpsuit covered in sand. Her technicians hurried over to help her.

They all gathered around the cool oasis as the leaderboard flashed up the final names and scores.

Jimmy went over to give Missy a high-five. She had a smile on her face wider than the Outback! She had ten points for the win. Jimmy had eight points for coming in second, and Horace had six for his third place. Horace stood apart from the rest of the group, his arms crossed in annoyance at losing out on first place. Jimmy moved on to congratulate Chip, who had managed to walk away with four points. Sammy was happy with his two points, and Princess Kako didn't get anything for her last place, but the crowd gave her a huge round of applause for managing to finish.

Then Missy climbed on the podium and received her sash for first place, and a bottle of fizzy juice. While it was tradition to shake it up and spray the crowd and her fellow racers, Missy had her own way of celebrating.

"There's no way I'm wasting this!" she shouted.

She stood and drank half the bottle in one go, burped loudly and tipped the rest over her own head. The crowd and her competitors laughed and cheered. "Ah, that's better!" she boomed.

Out of the corner of his eye, Jimmy could see a sulky Horace storming away from the podium towards Monster. Horace frowned at the colossal machine, and angrily kicked one of her massive tyres.

"Ooowww!" he screamed, hopping up and down as he stubbed his toe on one of the gigantic wheels. Jimmy could see his mouth moving rapidly as he hurled insults at Missy's robot racer, shouting rude words that thankfully couldn't be heard over the cheers for Missy.

Jimmy chuckled as Horace gritted his teeth and held his toe.

"Stupid robot!" Horace hissed.

In reply, Monster unleashed a cheeky jet of compressed air from her exhaust, and sent Horace flying high into the air! He landed in the calm blue water of the oasis, and sat up, coughing and spluttering in outrage.

"That should cool him off!" Jimmy said with a grin.

CHAPTER FIFTEEN
Fan Mail

As he stood on the second-place spot on the podium, waving to the crowds, Jimmy saw a head of white hair pushing its way towards him.

"Well done, Jimmy! I knew you could do it!" Grandpa shouted as he reached his grandson. Jimmy leaped off the podium and down into the crowd where Grandpa gathered him up in a hug. They moved away from the pack of journalists so they could talk.

"Thanks, Grandpa. It wasn't the same without being able to talk to you. It was so scary not being able to ask you for advice."

"But you did it, didn't you? That's my boy!" said

Grandpa, ruffling Jimmy's hair. "What happened at the start today? You all went off in totally the wrong direction for an hour!"

Jimmy told him about the faulty compasses and his suspicion that Horace had tampered with them. "Which reminds me..." Jimmy said, telling Grandpa what he'd overheard outside Horace's tent.

"Why, that no-good, dirty Pelly family! I'll see that they never race again! They should have points docked! I'll make sure—"

"But Grandpa, we've no proof!" Jimmy interrupted. "Horace and Mr Pelly are too sly, anyway. They'll have covered their tracks." Jimmy was sure that the Pellys would deny it if they were asked about it, and they had probably already thrown the device away to cover themselves. They were not great racers, but they were *really* good at cheating.

"We've got to do *something*," Grandpa said angrily. "It's unfair! It's unjust! It's an outrage!"

"Well we could always tell Lord Leadpipe..." Jimmy suggested.

"That buffoon! He couldn't fix a problem with a toolkit the size of Cabbie—"

Grandpa was interrupted by a huge fanfare announcing the arrival of Lord Leadpipe.

"Here we go," said Grandpa, rolling his eyes. "Let His Highness speak!"

"Dear fellow Robot Races enthusiasts!" said Lord Leadpipe, his voice bellowing around the oasis through the stacks of amplifiers. "I must extend congratulations to Missy McGovern and her robot Monster for a well-fought battle over the last two days, and a well-deserved first place!"

Everyone applauded, except for the Pelly family.

"And well done to all our competitors, who shall enjoy a good rest aboard my luxury airship before reaching *new heights* in the next leg of the competition!"

Jimmy frowned. *Was that a clue?* he wondered.

Lord Leadpipe busied himself with interviews, his arm around a grinning Missy.

"Look at him!" said Grandpa. "Did I ever tell you about how he nicked my life's work? And how he made off with my best clipboard...?"

Jimmy hid a grin. "Anyway, what about the Pellys?" he asked.

"They are no good rotten scoundrels, those two," said Grandpa indignantly. "We might not be able to change the results, but you beat them fair and square. And don't you worry, my boy. They'll get their comeuppance. Cheaters never prosper—" Grandpa stopped talking suddenly and his cheeks went bright red. Then he muttered, "Um, anyway, better go and check Cabbie's radiator temperature." And with a nervous glance over Jimmy's shoulder he started to hurry off.

Jimmy turned to see what his grandpa was looking at, and saw Bet Bristle cutting through the crowd of journalists. *No wonder he's gone red!* thought Jimmy. *Grandpa's always had a little crush on Bet!*

"Good day, Mr Roberts!" said Bet, calling after Grandpa.

Grandpa blushed again and stammered a reply. "G-good day, Ms Bristle. I'm, er, just needed elsewhere. Time to hose Cabbie down and get him ready for his photocall. He hates looking dirty for the cameras!" Grandpa disappeared, leaving Bet looking confused.

"Jimmy! Well done on another fantastic race!"

she said, pushing a microphone under his nose. Her cameraman stood behind her, zooming in to Jimmy's face.

"Thanks, Bet. I was beginning to wonder if we'd make it back at all."

"Tell me, Jimmy, how did you cope with the heat and the sand? Have you learned anything for the next race?"

"I think we'll all be glad to see the back of the desert!" He laughed. "The next race? I'm just going to make sure we pack plenty of ice cream."

"Ah-ha! Of course!" laughed Bet. "I've always described you as the underdog, but that's not really the case now."

"What do you mean?"

"You've done so well that you're now one of the favourites to win the competition!" said Bet, her smile widening. "You're now top of the leaderboard, and your fan ratings have gone through the roof! Surely you know all this? We've had hundreds of enquiries from companies asking if you are looking for new sponsorship."

Jimmy shook his head. He thought that it looked

as though he was being modest, but it was true. He'd never really thought about having fans before.

"We're cooped up in that airship all week. We don't really get to see that side of the races," he said.

"Ah, yes, that reminds me!" said Bet. She stuck her fingers in her mouth and whistled loudly like an army sergeant. "We've got something for you."

A Robo TV employee came running, dragging a large sack behind him.

"As the fans can't get hold of you while you're up on the airship all week, they send all their fan mail to us at Robo TV. This sack is just one week's worth, and doesn't include all the messages we get on our website."

Jimmy was astonished. He picked out a few letters and opened them to find out what people could possibly be writing to him for. There were letters from teenagers, drawings from kids in primary schools, photos of fans with banners they had made. There was even one from an elderly lady who said watching the races was the highlight of her week. The letters were from all over the world!

"This is incredible!" he said. "Thanks, everyone! I'll

make sure I read every letter."

Just then there was another fanfare and Bet was forced to cut their interview short as Lord Leadpipe took to the stage again.

"My dear friends! I couldn't let the opportunity go by to get you all to take part in one last race here in the desert."

Jimmy couldn't believe it. Another race? Cabbie wouldn't be ready to race again just yet.

"But fear not! You won't be needing your trusty mechanical mates this time. No, I shall provide your transport. This shall be very special. Very special, indeed!" Lord Leadpipe giggled like a schoolboy. "I am proud to announce the very first Leadpipe Industries' Camel Derby!"

CHAPTER SIXTEEN
Horace Gets the Hump

The course that Lord Leadpipe had prepared was a simple one. Once around the oasis, grab a flag from a post 400 metres out in the desert, and back again. First across the finish line was the winner, and would receive a brand-new, top-of-the-range 3D gamer phone from Leadpipe Industries.

Jimmy thought it sounded like it was a good deal, until he saw the camels up close. They were huge! Not to mention smelly, loud and a bit unpredictable.

"I hear the trick to riding a camel is to become one with it," said Lord Leadpipe, as though he were an expert.

The cameras and crowd gathered around, laughing as each of the participants approached the camels. Chip and Kako went up to them slowly, looking scared of the giant things. One camel turned to see what was going on, moving its dozy expression and long eyelashes over to the racers. Kako turned and fled, screaming as she ran. Chip managed to mount his camel, but nearly fell off as it stood up. Cameras flashed as he hung on for his life, the crowd laughing.

Missy was full of confidence after her win, and she charged up to the camel and took it by the reins. "I've been riding horses since I was four. It can't be much different!" she exclaimed.

Sammy approached his camel and coolly hopped on its back. "I love camels!" He pulled on the reins and the camel turned obediently round in a circle. The crowd applauded, and Jimmy laughed.

"Not fair! They don't have many camels in Smedingham," he joked.

He saw Horace trying to clamber on his less-than-trusty steed. Horace was perched on the camel rocking back and forth, shouting "GO!" and "MOVE!" The camel stayed where it was, sat under a tree in the shade. "I think mine's broken!" he called.

Jimmy glanced over and noticed that the camel was chewing on something that looked remarkably like one of Grandpa's famous jam sandwiches. The camel appeared to be enjoying it enormously!

He looked round and caught Grandpa's eye in the crowd, who winked back. So that's what he was up to!

Jimmy looked at his camel, and supposed he should try to get on it. The handler handed him the reins, and he awkwardly climbed on. They lined up at the start, and Lord Leadpipe took up his position with a starting pistol.

"On your marks ... get set ... go!" he shouted with a bang.

The camels were off in a shot – all except for Horace's, which stubbornly stayed put. Jimmy could see Sammy out in front looking like a professional jockey, with Missy just behind, doing a good impression of one. Jimmy was bouncing along in third place, and he turned to see Kako and Chip trotting along behind him. They were running fast, but nearly falling off from bouncing around so much.

"Theeeeeeseeeee thiiiiiiiiiings aaare soooooooooo

shaaaaaaaakkkyyyyyy!" called Chip, his teeth rattling loudly.

They ran once round the oasis and then out into the desert. Luckily, Jimmy's camel seemed to know where it was going so he didn't have to do much steering. He spotted the pole with the flags up ahead and leaned out to grab a flag, just seconds after Sammy and Missy had grabbed theirs.

Turning their camels back round towards the oasis, they hit the final straight. Sammy was charging out ahead like it was a normal Sunday morning ride in the park for him, while Missy seemed to be making all the right movements and noises to encourage her camel to the finish line.

"Come on camel!" Jimmy yelled, "if you win this you can have all the jam sandwiches you can eat!"

Jimmy flicked the reins and clicked his tongue and suddenly his camel sped forward like it had Cabbie's nitro-blaster rockets attached to its side!

Before he knew it, Jimmy had passed Missy and a confused-looking Sammy to take first place! The crowd went crazy! He climbed down from the camel, and bowed at the applause from the audience.

It wasn't quite the win that he wanted to get that day, but he was pleased to win the new phone.

He glanced back over to the start line where Horace sat alone on his camel. He scowled at the animal, which turned its head round to face him and spat into the sand below.

"Move, you stupid thing!" shouted Horace. But his camel sat down again and promptly fell asleep.

After the long, hot race, everyone was keen to relax and enjoy themselves. They celebrated with an evening of music, dancing and a great feast. Cabbie made so many ice creams that he joked he'd turn into an ice cream van.

Finally it was time to go. Lord Leadpipe's airship hung above the oasis, casting a welcome shadow over the crowds, who were beginning to wind their way back to the shuttle airships that would take them all home.

Jimmy drove Cabbie into the gigantic workshop in the centre of the airship, where the other robot racers were parking their robots.

"That was some race!" said Chip. "I sure hope the next one is as exciting!"

"I bet Leadpipe has got something up his sleeve," said Missy. "Nothing we can't handle, though. Isn't that right, Kako?"

"Too right, mate!" said Kako, sounding like Missy. The princess yawned and then said, "I'm going to bed. I could sleep for a month after that race!" Then without another word, she and Missy both walked off to their cabins.

"Where is Horace?" asked Sammy. "He bet his boots that he would win, remember? I wanted to make sure he would hand them over."

"He's in the shower," said Jimmy. "He stepped in a puddle of camel wee back at the oasis, and he's cleaning himself off. You might not want those boots."

Sammy pulled a face. "OK, maybe not. You are going to bed?"

Jimmy was shattered, but he didn't want to sleep just yet. He shook his head. "I'll see you in the morning. I've got some stuff to do."

While all the other teams headed for their rooms,

Jimmy spent time doing the thing he loved doing best – giving Cabbie a good wash and chatting with Grandpa. They talked about the adventures they'd had already in the competition, Grandpa's trick with the jam sandwiches and what might be their next challenge.

"Hey, Wilf! I'll need a new set of shock absorbers for the next race," said Cabbie. "The ones I've got now creak a bit."

"I know the feeling, Cabbie!" Grandpa replied. "My knees are playing up something awful. You must be getting old too!"

Jimmy gave Cabbie a squirt of soapy water, and the robot gave him a playful squirt back with his windscreen washers.

"Hey! We should fit a hot-chocolate maker," Jimmy suggested. "We could be sent to a cold country next!"

"Hmm, we'll see," said Grandpa. "Let's find out what sort of race Loony Leadpipe has got in store first." He leaned forward to look at Cabbie's windscreen. "You missed a bit."

They scrubbed and polished Cabbie into the night, joking, bickering and laughing all the time. Cabbie soon looked as good as new – apart from the rust holes, of course. But Jimmy liked those. Cabbie's bodywork shone and his alloy wheels gleamed, and Jimmy sat down on the wet floor with his grandpa, a mug of tea in his hand and a smile on his tired face.

"You know what, Grandpa? We're a great team. That goes for you too, Cabbie!"

"Thanks, Jimmy!" said Cabbie.

"I mean it. I wouldn't want to be racing with any other robot, or with any other engineers. I feel like we can win this whole competition!" Jimmy said.

"Of course we can!" said Grandpa. "We're Team Jimmy! Whatever the next race has in store, we'll be ready for it!"

Jimmy and Grandpa clinked their mugs together in a toast, and drank to the future. Around them the airship hummed and the engines purred, powering them on to the next destination and another amazing stage of the Robot Races.

ROBOT RACES

RESULTS TABLE

RACE 4: DESERT DISASTER

Race Position	Racer	Robot	Points
1	Jimmy	Cabbie	26
2	Missy	Monster	24
3	Horace	Zoom	22
3-	Chip	Dug	22
5	Kako	Lightning	16
6	Sammy	Maximus	14

For more exciting books from brilliant
authors, follow the fox!
www.curious-fox.com